Now, Forever Yours

Or

Look Back for Love

Now, Forever Yours

Or

Look Back for Love

RAJESHWAR PRASAD

GYAN

Published by

Gyan Publishing House
5, Ansari Road
Daryaganj, New Delhi-110002
Phone: 011-47034999, 9811692060
E-mail: books@gyanbooks.com

Distribution Network
gyanbooks.com
India, USA, Canada, UK, Australia, France

ISBN: 978-93-7097-848-5 (HB)
First Published, 2025

Printed at: Gyan Press, Delhi.

Now, Forever Yours
Or
Look Back for Love

Author: Rajeshwar Prasad

DEDICATION

To all those who have embraced woes and tears –
Conjugal life was a tree of fears.
Who suffered too much and were mocked at –
By deeds and duty – time and fate – till date.
Alas, strife and domestic violence!
Oh, now, love all to them! Peace, peace, peace!

Contents

Preface

Love's adoration like a mystic seer
Through vision looks at the invisible,
In earth's alphabet finds a godlike sense;
But the mind only thinks, "Behold the one
For whom my life has waited long unfilled,
Behold the sudden sovereign of my days."

– Savitri: Sri Aurobindo

Love is neither produced in fields nor bought from markets, love is neither found in sexual practices nor any other lustful activities. Love is wonderful and religious, and only the Lord can enjoy its flavours. The lover and the beloved are both spiritual. In this vein of love, the beloved may become the lover, and the lover may become the beloved.

For love's sake, The Lord Himself is made two to taste love. However, it is very obvious that there are some worldly unaware individuals who lack the understanding of the actual meaning of the word "love" and see lust as the word in place of "love". Lust is easily observable in all living beings, especially among friends, devils, demons, ghosts, etc. However, the reality is that only free souls should be loved.

In intimacy, a believer longs to give up all to the Lord without an expectation of reward. Love is free from delusion and pain and involves emancipation and infinite bliss. Love has an air of releasement and emancipation. The Lord becomes a slave to the deity who abides in love. Love makes every passing moment good and grants us ecstasy, and love is uncovered by the happiness felt towards the object of affection.

Procreation is the highest of men's undertakings, and sex organs are for procreating the function of procreation which is to extend the Creation. The Creation is absurd without a man. If procreation is fair, the world will be fair. So, everyone must work through the issues of love, sex, and marriage fairly.

Marriage is the most pious institution in society. It is the organisation that society has constructed and endorsed as a device for normality of production. There are different systems of marriage in different societies. But one thing is common to all these marriages. It is an agreement between two sexes from different genders for sexual intercourse over an extended period. This sexual intercourse leads to the birth of children. Marriage is not only for sexual intercourse, but rather it also involves human sacrifice. And if there is no human sacrifice, the marriage institution has no meaning.

Society is an invention of mankind, to control mankind all for the good of mankind. Man is a social being and who regards it, lives in peace and rest because one gets its support. However, those who do not pay attention to it are small and constrained and have to bear their whole life. Society itself is a free-of-cost balm for all mankind. It gives everything to live happily and costs nothing.

At present, lakhs of cases exist in the courts of law based on the Domestic Violence Act, Dowry Act, and Maintenance Act. It is obvious that certain individuals who travel to the court of law in search of justice are wasting their precious years of life, and they are getting something less meaningful than the satisfaction and the joy of life because their precious time of life is continuing to go by in conflict. The courts of law or any other entity cannot bestow love, joy, peace, and rest on anyone unless that person lacks virtue and understanding. Thus, every person has to take virtues, which can offer love, peace, rest, and happiness in life.

One shouldn't forget that there is no such human being in the world who is not trouble-ready. Marital life can bring some difficulties, but they are easily solved by knowledge. It is, indeed, a very memorable thing to be told that human virtues are even more effective weapons than all of the other weapons in the world, which could put an end to bad discrimination.

In the boundless ocean of thought, the content things in it are too little but very practical, and man should think to himself about the act of his life. It is not to be overlooked that small chains together constitute a large barricade and several small, but strong, habits lead to a giant man. Life is esteemed by virtues and not by wealth and that life is accredited in the value that Creation has given, the life attributed to Jesus Christ, Lord Buddha, Lord Mahavira, Guru Nanak, Lord Rama, Lord Krishna, Lord Gandhi and others.

Rajeshwar Prasad

Chapter - 1

Lovers' Own Country

Arran was an exceptionally good son for his parents, Bali and Dali. They loved him with every breath of their life. He had just entered his teenage. He used to read Daniel Defoe's *Robinson Crusoe* and, in all of its incredible details, found himself captivated by the life of an adventurer such as Crusoe, caught between cannibals, captives and mutineers, before being rescued. He also suggested his classmates read it.

But now he was changed. This novel seemed meaningless to him. So, he began to read books of romantic stories. Whenever he had time, he would go to the bookshops where he bought such books. He kept it secret and used to read in private hours. None of this was apparent to his parents or his teachers.

Romantic books not only improved his state of mind but also improved his character. He had already previously won some awards in school for his academic achievements. But now it had become a thing of the past.

He was pleased to notice the charm of Abby, the only child of Lara and Doran. She was charming. So, they loved her heartily. She read in the same school that Arran read. He would always watch her very intensely every time he met her. He would get lost in thought, and wondering when and how to tell Abby of his love.

Since they attended the same school, they also often ran into each other in that commonplace. Arran was two years older than Abby. They used to see one another whenever they met and wished to say something, but in the lack of private time, they controlled their passions.

One day, a new event of love occurred. Arran once saw Abby alone at the main gate of the school. Seeing her, he fell in love at first sight. He was lost in thinking about her beauty. He stood there and looked at her from head to toe, not even remembering anything. His feet stopped there as it was chained.

He spontaneously, from the language in his tongue, spoke, warm and slow, saying, "I love you."

She heard him with interest, but she did not reply immediately. After that, there was a brief dialogue between them in the form:

"Aha, Abby! I love you, my darling. Do you not see me? It is me."

"Who?"

"Arran."

"In which class do you read, Mr Arran?"

"I am two years senior to you."

"To which colony do you belong?"

"I belong to Whites Colony..., and you?"

"I belong to Sweet Lake."

"I fell in love with you at first sight. I love you. Seeing your blissful charm, my heart began to thrill my pulse began to beat fast.

"Now I am in a hurry. I am already late."

"Okay."

This brief talk between Abby and Arran came after several future events. They exchanged their phone numbers. They became friends on *Facebook*. They chatted on it regularly. Arran showed deep and lasting love for her and made the effort to express to her how he felt, hoping to win her heart, and Abby remained his emotional crutch.

After this short discussion, he was sure that he would win her and was too eager to have sex with her. He used to daydream about her and they both wanted her to be around him. Sometimes, he became restless for seeing her face and her charming body. From time to time he would dream at night, seeing her and her face would appear and shimmer before him. He did not give too much attention to the subject but often used to think about her. He fancied himself in touch with her private organs. He imagined how pleasant her sex organ would be! He made a comparison of her beauty with that of other girls and rated her as "the prettiest". He also pictured how she would look stripped naked in his arms and how she would exhibit her inner beauty. He recalled her appeal and beauty and knew she was 'one of the best in the world's top ten'.

In contrast, Abby was in no Great Hurry as Arran was. She never said, 'yes'. She thought to know him in different manners his conduct and his family background. So, she did not express her inner feelings. So, therefore, she was just filling up her time and she used to tell us "heh" or "no". Or she kept silent. But her love was hidden in her silence, or in 'heh' or in 'no'.

Arran also understood all this of Abby and the general nature of girls. He tried hard to win her heart. However, she was calm and still and wanted to understand the extent of Arran's love.

Arran was chained with her emotionally. He'd sometimes ask her to go to the park or the cinema hall by herself. However, she would not and went to see it with one or more of her friends, or her cousin Susan. Knowing that she had stepped out of her house, he tracked her whereabouts and made the ultimate effort to prove his depth of love. He even sometimes wandered into her neighbourhood looking for a glimpse of her from next door.

He once wrote her a love note, which she gladly took. Reading the letter, her attitude was sweet, never revolting. Whatever her response was, she never saw him just her own way. So, Arran tried to know her attitude about whether she loved him or not, but it was not disclosed by her in any way.

Abby never said, 'yes', but her heart was not as plain or empty as was in the past. When she knew that Arran loved her, her heart was coloured with romance. She said nothing but used to think about him and his love for her. However, she left her testament a secret, and the way of her heart was locked. If Arran followed Abby often, she would think about him and be excited to go. Her heart was flooded with the passions of love and sex. But her love was cool and silent sweet and secret. She regarded him as one of her choices. She was absorbed in thinking when she imagined him. She used to become passionate. Sometimes, she became restless. On occasion, she couldn't have a free choice over her sexual drives. But she anyhow controlled herself. Sometimes, she dreamt at night that she was having sex with Arran.

On the other hand, Arran's condition was considerable. He tried to keep up with her, but she was out of his sexual grasp. He attempted to manifest his affection in many ways, however, she wasn't rushing, and she therefore didn't let him kiss or touch her body. Being unable to resist the temptation to conquer her affection, he used to stay near the school's main gate and with a deep-hearted smile would watch her passing by. He wanted to know her by himself to give her the best ideas in a little time.

At times they shared course books to alleviate their sexual desires. Sometimes, they exchanged their important notes for examinations. While taking these materials, they touched their fingers to one another. In this manner, they sought the consolation of their love and maintained their union. However, the most defining work of intimate relations, which is best enjoyed together amongst each other, is yet to come.

On the day of festivals, Arran tried to meet her in any way, and he used to present festive gifts to her. She did so, too, but she was cold and silent on the surface to have sex with him when he was agitated and restless and wanted to do it as soon as he could, which he did by following her running skirt no matter where she went whenever and wherever she went.

Abby once went to her maternal aunt's home and he also knew it. That is he meant to grab and he went there as well. He realised that she needed to attend the cinema hall with her cousin, Susan. For example, he also got there at an earlier hour and queuing to get a ticket for him.

While, in the meantime, Abby and Susan arrived and found a line stretching out for purchasing tickets. Abby also observed Arran in a queue, but Arran didn't perceive her. She was already late.

So, she met Arran and requested to buy tickets for her and Susan. He willingly undertook the task and purchased the tickets. She was covering the cost of the ticket, but no he refused to pay it. Abby and Susan thanked him and praised him for his kind cooperation and gentle-mindedness.

Buying tickets, they entered the cinema hall. They sat together and Arran sat beside Abby as was suggested by her cousin. Abby had already told Susan that he loved him. So, it was quite known also by Susan.

He also bought peanuts, soft drinks, coffee, and then to eat during the show. In the meantime, Arran wished to kiss her, but it was not allowed by Abby. They were zealous, and she just sat, leaving his one hand resting near her thigh for a while. He was also very eager to close her, but she let him in the hen. Nonetheless, her cousin told her that she should have a good time with him on the balcony if she loved the boy. However, she stated that she was not in a rush.

When the show was over, they went to a restaurant. There they indulged in chocolate cream, and Arran made the sacrifice cheerfully. He refused to let them pay even one cent to purchase anything. He also got the bus tickets for both of them and bade them farewell on the bus that took them to their house, too. They further agreed to meet again the following week at the zoo.

They departed thereafter eating chocolate cream and reached home. Arran went to his home alone. While departing, Arran gave a love letter, which she took gladly. Drinking at home, she read it and also (by reading it) showed it to her cousin. The letter was highly romantic as follows:

"Aha, Abby! Aha, the princess of my dream! I look at so, so many, yet you are but one in my eyes. Whatever I see, I find you in all this. I see you on the pages of books always when I read. The day I eat, I see your smiling visage on the plate. When I sleep, I see you in a dream while sleeping, I see your image. In the water and sky, I still only see your picture. It is an immortal odour from your body that I would like to experience. I do not find such a smell anywhere. What smell in me, I don't tell! Immortal! When I touched you, the smell was transferred to me. It is still in me. I feel it. I picture your inner beauty, which is something I want to savour. But you are lingering unnecessarily. Do you not want to bring me somewhere private where we can go all out? We will enjoy our privacy. There was an immortal feeling when I was close to you and I saw your rosy cheeks and charming beauty. They were like immortal fruits. I want to kiss you a thousand and a thousand times. When I saw you, it seemed that you were a magnet. I was implicitly being passed at you as a whole..."

Susan also read this love letter and said to Abby that he really loved her. She suggested she marry him. However, Abby also stated that she did not rush it so the idea that girls should take it at their own pace was also applicable here. Thus, she considered everything properly as she could.

Following their pre-plan, they gathered at the zoo a week later. For it, Arran bought tickets. In the meantime, Arran and Abby were only there. Susan had not come as she was ill. She talked to Arran about her ailment, and he showed pity and sympathy for her. He also wanted a speedy restoration to health for which he also prayed to God. Abby felt that he was too kind and gentle, so he was showing such humane passion for her cousin. So, she thanked him for his pity and sympathy. They saw the animals in the zoo and enjoyed it. They saw a pair of deer, and they were doing sex acts. Seeing them, they also became sexually passionate and romantic. Having examined all the exhibits within the zoo, they perched on a bench by themselves and whispered romantically:

Arran said, "What a great romantic scene! Think about this pair of deer. How much they were enjoying! Why can we not do this? Why are we lingering to enjoy heavenly pleasure? We should not waste our valuable time. The time which passes never comes back. So, we should enjoy this time."

"Let the time come."

"When will a time come?"

"Time will answer. It is in the core of the future."

"We have to say."

"We have to follow only."

"We have to perform. Time will follow."

"Time follows none."

"Tell me!"

"Let it come."

"When…?"

"When God wishes to be done, all this."

"But…When…?"

"Do you feel that I am a cheater? I do understand your love for me. Wait for some time."

"Okay."

They ran to a nearby restaurant and shared snacks. Not to mention for sure they were incredibly happy to also be in the anticipation of achieving complete, sexual satisfaction soon. They promised to meet from time to time. After taking snacks, they went to their homes.

After weeks, Abby returned home to her parents with her parents. Arran lived normally and attended his classes usually. He was certain that at some point in time, he would be able to appreciate the physical attractions of Abby. He recalled her and the plan for winning her affection as soon as possible. He thought he was getting close to her privacy because she had consented to spend some time at the zoo by herself, and she had touched his hand by her leg for a few seconds. He often recalled the time when he was close to her intimate area.

Thus, some weeks passed. One day, a new event occurred. He was alone at home. He was solving his mathematical homework. He tried hard, but he failed to solve it because he was solving it half-heartedly and his attention was mainly focused on his romance with Abby. He nevertheless left the books and notebooks on the bookshelf and slowly began to reflect on his fascination for Abby.

In the meantime, he was lost in thinking. He was very serious and began to murmur. He mumbled that the world is the largest classroom where man learnt, all the time long. Man learned his whole life. But life without sexual enjoyment was meaningless. Studying without a girlfriend was meaningless. Sexual gratification during students' lives was a lot of wonderful joys in life. So, everyone should do this as maximum as possible. Who did not do so, was truly not a man he was a man without sense he was a misfortune number 'one'. But according to Arran, he was a man of great sense and pleasure, and he would not take rest till he won her and enjoyed her inner charm wholeheartedly. He believed that if he just tried to do it like that, she would end up understanding eventually his thoughts and agreeing to sex. He was sure. Other boys said the same matter. His friends talked that slowly and slowly girls came to the boys' lap. They did not come directly. Except for him, all of his friends had girlfriends. He had firm faith that she would come to his arms within some days. He knew its ways.

He used to think that if it happened, and she came naked to his arms, what a great matter of pleasure for him would be! Aha! What a fine thing of delight when his single hand rested upon her body! He considered that other boys had girlfriends but were not likeable as her, and she could grant him divine joy as she was as beautiful and sweet as a fairy. So, he should follow whatever she said. Then everything would be in his hands.

He thought, "Aha! How pleasant hours would be with her, in a private room when she would be fully naked in my arms before my eyes. Aha! Aha!"

He muttered the same which were inwardly active.

In contrast, Abby was, on the one hand, generally attending classes at the school, and her desire for love was being gently steered toward Arran. She was in no rush and a very measured answer was given her. The flow of passion was regulated, but she also loved him and desired to have intercourse with him immediately. She also thought about any other better options. Sometimes, it happened that when she sat to study, her attention was removed from there and moved toward her lover, Arran. Sometimes, she lost in thinking. Whenever she saw some girls loved or kissed by boys, she also wanted to be kissed and loved by anyone, who would satisfy her in the meantime.

She was fully aware of the fact that she was loved by Arran. However, she was also searching for a more desirable partner (i.e., a better partner) if applicable and optimal. However, in her view, Arran was the best of all the other boys in her group. She was convinced that one day she would be able to fall happily into Arran's arms and be loved more than the girls in her circle.

Chapter - 2

Love Becomes Too Hot

Abby has not revealed any secret of love to anybody but Susan, whose secret has remained concealed. One day, Abby was in her school. During lunchtime, students were dispersed hither and thither. There were some bushy and flowery parts in the school where some girls and boys used to eat. Abby was sitting there alone. In the meantime, Abby saw that a boy had taken a girl in his lap. She was agreeably kissed and embraced by her lover. The boy and girl were mutually in a deeply flirtatious state. They completely surrendered themselves before one another. The situation was highly romantic. In the meantime, there was a sweet and memorable discussion between them.

Thus, they enjoyed their privacy, feeling that no one was seeing all this. However, it was established that Abby was there. When she saw all this, she was excited, and it became intolerable for her. It was the preservation of sexual competence at a young age. This event shook her to make sex as a sexual act as early as possible. The sex force directly fired her. Then she wanted to do as they were doing in the bush. Meanwhile, she got into a sexual frenzy and wanted to make out with anyone. She envied the ability to do so with anyone else back then. She went home after school, and she was lost in thought.

She murmured. She muttered that she was a fool. She did not know life and its reality. Others enjoyed it, and she saw, though she had better chances...he had a better lover. She was a fool. She should do the same, as others were doing. What was wrong in doing so? One day, every girl had to do so...every girl had to open the door of sex. So, what was wrong in doing so now? All did so. She was better than them. She had a better option than them. Now she would also enjoy it, but after serious consideration, otherwise, she might have to repent like some others. Her mother used to say that one should do everything but consider its outcome. The change in her attitude, for instance, could therefore be readily grasped when she watched the school bush sex scenes.

Watching the romance she got as excited as though she wished to "shag" anyone she was able to, and not just Arran. This was the then condition of Abby. However, she exercised control over her desires, preferring to think through any love problem thoughtfully before engaging in sexual intercourse. She thus refrained from expressing her erotic urge and tried to have sex with anyone who would be more beneficial for her.

Conversely, all things about having sex with her carried great weight over Arran's mind, even though he suppressed his desires in hopes that he would eventually gain her and make the most of her brilliance in a pure, joyous, sexually unalloyed way. His bliss was hidden in expectations. So, he was too eager to gain her.

Meanwhile, Arran also learned that for the second time, Abby had gone to her cousin's house, for a holiday. He went there, too, and was greeted there, by her cousin warmly. Yet Abby said not to see him as her mother was also present. He also realised that she was not able to come to the place she agreed to because she was with her mother. So, he was not taking her behaviour as disregard for him. He thought that one day he would be able to love the delicious body of her just as others love the body of their sweetheart.

Here, her cousin's fare was not to be taken and nothing more could be done, but she wanted to help them because she understood the then condition and feelings of Abby, who was too eager to have sex with him or with anyone.

Arran was unable to be there, alas, but he was certainly keen. Thus, he thought of how to convey his message to her and he secretly wrote down a letter to be given to Abby's cousin in her name with the condition that she should not tell anyone about their love affair, and the letter was sent to her, as the letter was private and personal. Abby received the letter and read it by herself, but her cousin asked her to read the letter and said to her too, as the same. But Abby said that she was younger, and she would be out-routed by the exciting love letter. Abby also suggested to her cousin that she should not fall in love with anyone because it was a very terrible thing. She said that when one fell in love with anyone, he or she always used to think about sexual romances, not about any other works. At last her cousin confessed that she was younger, so she would not have read such a tender letter of the love story of Arran and Abby. The letter was very soul-stirring and was read by Abby by herself in this way:

"O my spirit! Believe me, I love you. I will die unmarried I will die unloved, but will never love anyone except you I will never marry any other except you. You must understand that I am hot to be loved I am ready to be loved. I have left to eat food in your name. It has become non-consumable for me. I always think about you how you are...where you are...what are you doing. My life without it is now a weight on my shoulders. I cannot live without you. I expect that you will understand my feelings. I expect you will reply soon. Should be handed over to my cousin in your name and I will get it from her next Sunday. Think a little! Imagine! How pleasant our journey of love will be! "

This letter was read by Abby. Reading the letter, her pulse began to beat fast. Her heart began to thrill. She was overwhelmed with the passion of love. She felt intensely, but she thought of it, of reality, of the world. Thus, she was taking her step toward Arran very carefully. She considered his letter and his interests and wished to be close to him tenderly.

Arran was waiting for a reply to his letter. Abby had read the letter but an answer was not received by Arran. He came there the next Sunday, but her cousin told him that no letter had been given to her by Abby for delivering to him. When Arran knew that no letter had been written in his name by Abby, he became sad and began to think that perhaps she did not love him. He knew that he had more maybe a year to have her heart, but he fell short. So, he was too nervous. He thought that perhaps he was no man of use to the girls. He was also unliked by her and all the other girls. He also thought that most of his classmates talked about their beloveds and most of them had beloveds, though he had no beloved while he tried hard to win Abby. So, he was inferior to them. He felt that he was not in a situation to show his face to anyone, while other boys discussed their love affairs with their beloveds and asked him about his beloved. But he said nothing because he had nothing to say about his romance.

Arran was nervous. In the meantime, a new event occurred. Arran was heavily shocked. On the occasion, some boys were found to be sitting on the school grounds and making conversation over their sweethearts. In the meantime, Arran was sitting there. They also inquired about his soulmate and his dating life.

They asked him, "Everything is forgotten when we enjoy the privacy of one another. Sorrows change into joy. Winter is changed into spring. Cold becomes heat. Tell us Arran, what are the results of you touching your beloved with your hands on their genitals? Have you no manliness?"

Arran was shocked by listening to them. He wanted to leave that place, but they ridiculed him and told him to stay in that place. So, he was sitting there uninterestingly. He said nothing. He was shamed among them. So many ideas began to come into his mind and heart. He was then very serious. Now his behaviour also changed, and he no longer wished to wait for her. He began to murmur.

He thought that he had no manliness. So, he should die. It would be then better for him. Except for him, all other classmates had beloveds, but he had no beloved. He was cheated. They got the affections of their sweethearts, God only respects! He didn't know. He used to speak sweet words to her, but until now she did not allow him even to kiss her rosy cheeks. How could he understand that she loved him? Perhaps she did not love him and she loved any other. Now it had become clear. She never said, 'yes'. She always misguided him. It was not too much change in the film hall to make out and enjoy, in the first class it was a dark and private cubicle, in which we were sitting. Her cousin had no objections. She was a gentle and kind girl. She was very helpful and understood their passions. The fact that, for the reason of the separate cabins, he had purchased tickets for this class only. Every time the opportunity arose, he would make the effort to win her affection, yet she was resolute that he could not get near her. So, he should not live in this world. He should commit suicide having consumed poison. He would make him immortal in this way. If he died in her name writing a suicide note, then the world would remember him that he loved her but had been cheated by Abby. When Abby finds out know his suicide and the suicide note in the name of the world that he had been cheated by her, she is shamed and commits suicide. Later on, we would meet in heaven, where we would enjoy one another. Now, this was the only way left to him. The next day, he would consume poison. All these concepts were hunting in his skull and his soul.

All this shows how boys and girls commit suicide. Now the situation of Arran was very considerable. He had become passive at the hands of sexual passion. He had forgotten what was expected by the parents who had given birth to him and the world which gave everything for the life of anyone.

Arran was therefore not in the position to wait it out and wanted a "Do or Die" approach. The next day he went to the market and purchased four tablets of poison sold in a shop of insecticides. When he arrived home, he went for a pen and paper to write the suicide note. Later on, he came to the temple to worship so that his soul could go to heaven after his suicide. In the temple, there was a vacant place where nobody was there and he wrote as follows, a suicide note:

"O my spirit, Abby! I adore you, but you do not love me, which has become obvious. I put a lot of effort into capturing your heart in various ways but to no avail. Whatever you think about me you are the only one in my heart whom I love. My situation has become critical, since the moment that I came to school, I watch my friends talk about their relationship with their special somebody, and I am without a special somebody. They also mock me. They say that I have no manliness they say that I am womanly. At this point, what am I supposed to do in this world? Now, what is the meaning of my life? I know there is no meaning. I tried enough to win your heart. Now, how I can live...how can show my face to my classmates? They are proud of their beloveds but for which thing, I will show my pride. So, I should die. But I will wait for you in heaven and will see you from the railings of heaven. When you arrive, I will welcome you in advance and we will dine in Heaven under the great Green Tree where we will finally, heartily eat. We will never come back here. Within a few minutes I am heading to the hill opposite the fountain, where there is an isolated spot for such activities and young boys and girls are still conducting such activities. Yours... Arran..."

He wrote the suicide letter and hid the letter in the inner pocket of his shirt and decided to commit suicide on the hillside by the fountain.

Holding it, he stepped back to the side of the main doorway of the temple. He begged God for a happy departure from the world to heaven and a place in heaven. After prayer, he moved back to come out. But as he moved back, the forefront touched Abby, who had come to the temple for prayer. Intransitively, subconsciously, her body came into contact with his chest in the crowd. They looked at one another faces. Abby asked Arran to wait for her until she got back from prayer when she intended to talk to him. But it was felt by Arran that a great life force entered his body, which came from her breasts. He was surprised, to see this miracle. He thought that she had perhaps seen him coming to the temple, so she had followed him and came to the temple. He also found that he had consciously made contact with his chest using her body as a support. He thought that perhaps her thoughts had been changed. He was relaxed, and his mood changed within minutes. The sense of despair changed into expectations forefront and forehanded. He further felt that this miracle was only possible by the blessings of God's way. He became happy, and he waited for her near the main gate of the temple. He looked about, hither and thither, to see if anyone was around her. He discovered that none was with her and she arrived alone at the temple to pray in the new attire.

After some minutes, she came to him, having worshipped deities. In the meantime, there was a sweet and serious discussion between them as follows:

"Have you got it?"

"What?"

"The same which you expected!"

"What?"

"The same which binds us to the bound!"

"No. None has given it to me."

"It was before your eyes."

"Where?"

"Bliss under the foot."

"I don't understand."

"Have you not seen this line on the bench upon which you sit in the classroom?"

"Yes, this sentence was dictated in the bench where I am sitting, but I don't know why."

"What is its meaning?"

"Bliss will be under the feet of your seat, and you can get up there."

"Please make it clear."

"The love letter!"

"Okay."

"I am in a hurry."

"Why?"

"My mother is waiting for me at the car parked in the courtyard of the shrine. She may see us. We will discuss it later."

Saying this, she departed from there. Following the discussion, a combined change in mood occurred and Arran abandoned his intention to commit suicide. The sense of joy overflowed his body from bottom to top. He was pleased, to see such a miracle. He so desired to go to school the following day to collect the love letter; otherwise, other guys may get it. His mind was then full of fancies. He was as friendly and happy as it has ever been. There was a sweet smile on his face. His mind was full of different ideas, and he thought about how God had saved his life forehanded, though he had not disclosed to her or anyone that he was going to commit suicide.

He left the suicide note wasted, and the tablets of poison thrown away and he happily reached home. He solved his homework. He seemed sweet and calm. Also, his parents asked him about what must have made him so calm, but he replied that he was normal.

The following day, he got up to school first and took off the foot of the desk. As he withdrew, he saw a bit of paper, which he picked up. He kept it in his purse and hid it so that no one could see it, and thought to read it when no one would be in the classroom. At lunchtime, when he was there by himself in the park, right at the spot he remembers having watched a boy and a girl stealing peace, to enjoy it alone together. He read the letter as follows:

"Bliss will embrace you soon..."

He read the letter, which was written on a piece of paper. A photograph of the surface of the heart was there upon which these sentences in fresh colourful letters, in red ink, were inscribed. It was small in dimensions, but dimension, yet crucially, of too great an importance that possessed the potential to bring joy in a life's relation. This letter was read by him frequently and gladly. He concealed this letter under his book and in the classroom he often found himself reading and seeing this letter even when the instructor was lecturing him. He pondered what is its meaning and believed that very shortly, he would be pleased with the inner beauty of Abby's lovely, soft and pretty body.

He exclaimed with joy and muttered. He felt that those five words of Abby's love letter were a godsend for him. After a long waiting period, hours of bliss would take place in his life and he would fully enjoy Abby's inner charm.

He said, "Aha! Aha! How pleasant would be the hours of bliss?"

He muttered about his private life he would see her inner charm he would see and enjoy her physical charm. She would be fully naked in his arms in a heavenly bed. He would sleep beside her. He would have sex acts with her. Its meeting occasions a lifelong (and lasting) happiness which will only cease at their demise, namely when their breath is ended. It seemed that in the next spring season when the stems would produce new leaves and flowers would bloom all around he would enjoy her bodily charm. Aha, bliss! Thus, he disclosed his heart in his muttering.

He was very happy. His happiness was easily visible on her face. He used to inscribe the fabric of happiness and satisfaction in the text of the imagination. He had forgotten totally that he was once going to commit suicide only because of Abby and his sudden meeting with Abby in the temple had saved his life and changed his mood. He considered himself a lucky man thinking that he was right falling in love with Abby, the most beautiful girl in the school. He also thought that others were not fortunate like him because their beloveds were not as charming as Abby. He was now normal. He used to attend school in a changed and happy state.

Thus, some months passed. In the city, there was a festival of the circus, known Imperial Circus. Most people used to enjoy it. Villagers and city boys both used to visit it in the evening show or the morning show. One day, Arran also went there to enjoy it. He got the ticket and entered the hi-fi class. On entering randomly he came across Abby her cousin in the same class, sitting together. Abby told me to sit close to her because some of the seats were empty next to her. So, Arran sat there, and he began to see the circus with them. During the show, some vendors of the circus used to sell some edibles and Arran used to buy all this. Just to do all of it, he served Abby and Susan to impress them. There was a wide impression of his conduct on them, and for this they thanked him. This was also a culture where, if there was a male/female split in a company, the cost was always borne by the males. So, Arran fulfilled this expectation and followed the culture. He continued to buy edibles and eat with them.

His impression was equally remarkable that Abby would have Arran consume edibles in a handkerchief in her lap, next to his thigh. Every time that he used it, he would try to feel her thigh and there was unvoiced agreement from Abby. It was also observed by Susan, who watched them with a smile, and who understood the true nature of the situation between them. Although she wished she did not stop them, she never attempted to interject. Arran thought that he was one step ahead in his love journey. So, he was very happy. Abby also wanted to be touched as maximum as he could, and she could passively. In the circus hall, there was no place to enjoy more privacy, but it was enough, and they felt the needs of one another. Their happiness was endless. Arran dreamed that if she went into his arms, he wouldn't mind her alone time.

Arran's happiness was uncontrollable. He got very excited and started to braid the strings of sexual gratification in and with Abby. It was a movement that was watched and enjoyed by Abby. His clothes were a bad fit, and so it was obvious to her. He masked it with a handkerchief, but it was still there.

Abby was also very glad. She conceived days, for example, when full satisfaction with him would be hers alone in a private room. She would have liked to follow Arran's wishes, but with no time for herself, it proved to be unthinkable.

Chapter - 3

Raging as a Subject

Some days passed. They resumed their gentle sexual activity, hoping to meet their hard romantic relationships shortly. Arran passed the Intermediate of Science examination after a few days and was graded in the first class. Its result was that his feet were not on the ground, but rather in the sky. His joyfulness was obvious in every step of his life. He began to build a castle in the air. The altitude record of his flight of achievement of Arran was greater than that of any other students from his class who have gone through with him. To tell his happiness was very difficult for him, not to mention guessing his dream.

Arran got very good marks in the examination. Thus, his parents too were very pleased and the love feast was grandly organized by them. They were there on the pavement, but their souls had become so accustomed to excitement...both physically, and emotively so. They started to draw the threads for Arran's glorious future. On the other hand, Arran was also thinking ahead in his way for his promising career. Some suggested he sit for the competitive examinations of the administrative service. Some suggested becoming a police officer – some said to be a doctor – different views by different persons. They explained that the school has a file with the record that at least four to five candidates passed each year in an administrative examination, so he should fill the file based on the tradition of the family. They also said that if he became an administrative officer, he would have maximum chances to prosper fast and earn enough money and he would get such a golden chance only if he held such a post.

Although, other students in the school were somewhat unhappy about the stance of the school. But they had no courage to go against the school administration to say anything against it. One brave student appeared in the media and freely expressed his thoughts.

He expressed that Arran was not a brilliant student. Questions posed to him in the course exams were tackled by the school teachers in another room surreptitiously, while Arran kept playing games on his mobile phone, which, alas, had its video recorder, and he was prepared to disclose it to the media. He had no hesitation – no fear. He stated that truth "is never disguised" and Arran had no special information on how to get good grades on the test, but he was, in fact, influential, and so, in the test, he employed improper methods. School authorities telephoned the experts in the field to answer his queries discreetly. Their special room was kept out of view, and in the absentee lists, he was listed as 'Absent,' but he signed it at the end of the session. All this had been done intentionally to highlight and upgrade him. This was also achieved when giving marks in viva voce and practical examinations. No officer checked him or any member of the flying squad searched or checked him. They reached the school and enjoyed cashew nuts, almonds, and expensive sweets with the school Principal. When they returned, they were given the sealed envelopes of money as a bribe. According to him, he had seen all this. He witnessed it several times. So, the degree of Arran was fake, and on the other hand, the degrees of other students were real degrees. But in this age of corruption all over the country, he had the maximum chance to get success in his life, and on the other hand, the meritorious students were compelled to suffer. He had enough money. His parents made money while others earned money. So, he bought marks he could buy degrees he could buy certificates. Several smokeless industries were running in the name of education centres all over India, and he could buy whatever he liked. However, some others had to find any reward in the blood and/or sweat. No matter how little, they had won, because of their effort. Hence he unveiled so many novel concepts before the Media on Arran and other areas.

There were different views of different people. Some were for and some were against it. Some students said he was a brilliant student and some said that he was an educational smart boy. This was a culture of becoming high status and thus eligible for the special privilege without taking the test to the table. There were not one, two, or three schools or colleges of this nature, but hundreds of thousands of educational institutes where all this was done so seamlessly and freely. Those students felt proud doing so, that they had such influence that they took the fruits without doing anything.

However, what was the true picture of Arran, that was unknown? Thus, one fortnight of Arran's happiness passed. The degree of joy went below and the preparation for the future went higher. He began to think about his next step, to get a degree. His parents thought to acquire a degree when aspiring to be a doctor, which would be appropriate when aimed at repairing human beings. So, Arran followed his parents' advice and became ready to do so. Thus, he was admitted to an institute which is an autonomous and self-subsided college. No competition – no waiting. He was admitted to that very private college of the same city then and there the college which was run by an education mafia who was also an influential political leader. He was the secretary of over sixty institutions of learning, and some were operating simply on the ledger.

Arran went to medical college as per class routine. He was pleased with the outcome of his decision that he would be a doctor. So, he attended his classes regularly. Professors were pleased with his work and during his four years of research, there were not any questions of indiscipline to appear before the institution.

In this way, the whole session passed. He passed medical tests and got the top position in the list of five with a grade of 'A+'. He fulfilled the hopes of his parents and others, and he came to them with his medical degree.

Having done it, Arran looked for a higher qualification for the work. He was enrolled in the same medical school as a *Doctor of Medicine*, for this reason. He began to attend the classes of the previous year very interestingly. Upon qualifying, for the preceding exams while progressing through the final year, happiness arrived to him as he moved into a rebellious role model for young boys. He was regarded as a pathfinder in the college. Students admired him for his practices and his new ways of raging. They praised him and said that he had got special training in raging and had crossed all the records. They declared that his name must be entered in the Book of World Records and that he would make the name of his homeland shine. He was held in high regard by the students for his ways, and he became his justice for the mad.

Arran was widely complimented for his running and psychics of the raging. He transferred to every department with some of his mates. He called some boys of the first year, or he approached them. Firstly, they laughed and befooled the boys. Later on, they got them naked among others, and did some immoral and inhumane acts. However, no ray of shame was on their countenance, and they raved about the ways of outbursts. All of this was part of Arran's and his friends' daily lives. It seemed that they had got a treasure of joy. Leaving their classes, they used to move in search of boys for raging. Raging was the main work of Arran and his friends, and the study was their secondary work. He liked it and roamed from department to department, to do so. He would even forget to eat and declared that the exercise of raging was a super meal for him. Treating himself as its inventor, since he had developed new directions of rage. At one time, other people employed some conventional methods, however, he started to employ contemporary technology for these purposes without feeling shame or fear. He also turned it into a work of business because some videos of raging were made with the help of high-grade mobile phones and sold in the market at high prices. It became a source of income for him and his friends. The police didn't take an interest in such issues to control them, as the crowd of boys and girls could create problems for them. The police tended to keep their distance rather than take an active participation in the matter. So, they freely practice the evils of raging. However, the government had ordered the department to take proper actions against such matters getting a matter of zero tolerance. But they applied a hundred per cent tolerance instead of zero per cent and idiot students frequently created problems for the college and some gentle students. The works of the study were severely impacted by the raging. Sometimes, some serious problems came to the district administration, some students were killed too.

Arran was overjoyed the next day, for he had given battle to a fair number of boys. It was also known by the media. So, the media also wanted to interview Arran. By the time Arran got to the hostel, he was recounting his methods of rage to a magazine editor, and the account was printed in that magazine.

He said delightfully that a bad temper is the most feasible work for character growth, and the last year of college brought him great joy. He said that the common people criticized it unnecessarily because they did not know its importance they were fully illiterate, uncultured, and rustic.

He said loudly, "How much pleasant the act of raging is! How humanistic and moralistic! It is very useful for college. Compulsory courses in raging should be included for each faculty. It is for their personality development. How would they know its significance? Political leaders and social activists condemn it unnecessarily. They will need to promote it – they will need to motivate it because it works in their total development, self-fulfilment, and happiness. The government has made a law to stop raging and prohibit raging, but it cannot be enforced by the government. However, who wrote the law – who understood the law? The legal instrument was enacted to adorn the Constitution and the parliament, and it did so. It was kept on the records. Let it remain on it. Let them pass. Let them criticize. They practiced their own raging laws without any kind of fear or shame. They said that they did not want to remain folk people like illiterate persons, and they did not want to live as old-fashioned and old-cultured human beings. They claimed to be modern in a modern world and not something 'dead or gone'. So, they did not like the education of the ancient age, which was fully meaningless. That was a hundred per cent stupid. What was at Nalanda University Vikramshilla University or Takshilla University? Was there raging? He was sure, there was no raging system. That is, education at those ancient universities was pointless."

Arran believed that if there is no raging, no education; if raging, complete education. Thus, Arran expressed his ideas very shamelessly.

He continued and expressed his ideas very proudly. He claimed that he had the feeling of pride, stating that he had experienced enough times of "raging". He was its expert – he was its master. He had invented all kinds of raging, which cannot be described nor uttered in words. Sometimes, the photographs of the private parts of the boys were stamped on paper. They were distributed among friends. The habit of masturbation was practiced in different ways.

On occasion, sexual acts and their positions were described in boys and they were performing the sexual acts. If they disobeyed us, they were tortured and beaten. Some boys or girls left the college for some time due to this culture, but whenever they came to the college, they had definitely to pass through the process of raging. No one was allowed to violate the virtue of raging. Who violated it, might be killed. They weren't entitled to live in this world and did not recognize it.

Doing so, he was very happy. He wished to do as maximum as he could. After some minutes he said again that…raging…raging…raging…People cried like crows unnecessarily. How much did it cost the federal and state purse? Not even a penny was given up in the practice of this virtue of impulsivity, which is to rage. Political leaders had no other work, so they discussed it in the house, which was meaningless. Social reformers, too, had nothing to reform; they, thus, sought the eradication of "overheated virtue. They did not know that it was a part of our education system for the all-round development of students. Those with ancient wisdom reproved it, and they viewed India in 10,000 BC. But students looked at India in 3000 AD. And they told them to cry, that they couldn't forget it, and would never forget humanity's virtue. The law was on the records. Who followed it? Who asked it? Did the law follow them? Let it lie on the records of the parliament."

Arran demonstrated that raging was good (that is, a virtue) rather than evil (that is, a vice). So, it should be freely practiced by them.

Not a single step backward was the girl's and the opposite was also true of the girl. They also wanted to speak with the media, but none were available. Anyhow, a woman journalist contacted the raging leader of the girls who became ready to interview, but on one condition that her name would not be disclosed. Her interview too was included with audio and published in the same magazine.

Raging's photographs were graphed and its video was also recorded by their mobile phones. In the meantime, our pleasure was uncontrollable and they felt the utmost pleasure. A few images and videos were additionally sold by them and they also generated income. They also observed and saw all this in their friends.

Doing all this, she began to laugh wholeheartedly. Other girls also laughed without any kind of shame. They began to praise their leader and said that she was their preceptor. They further reported that raging is a virtue, not a vice, and people who do not exercise this virtue in life are idiots.

She repeated that the following day they repeated the exercise. If the girl was not ready to do so, she was beaten and raged at by others by them forcibly.

Sometimes, they practiced the fabricated highly standard electronic equipment of the male and female private organs.

She said, "Aha! Aha, raging! How pleasant it was! Its rotation was 3000 rounds per minute. One could imagine how enjoyable it was! Very pleasing! Up and down!"

All this was done according to her will. She shared with that lady reporter, however, no sense of shame whatsoever. The media reported, and her pornographic writings were printed in the newspapers accompanied by reviews. On the other hand, hundreds of students criticized them and this evil. But, they lacked the courage to speak up and oppose the bad students – boys or girls. They criticized it and wanted its abolition at any cost. They recounted that they had endured too much because of this wickedness. Their position was also published in the newspapers, as listed below:

"...There are some inhuman practices still going on in this humanist age. Raging is one of them. This is one of those black spots in humanity and society. This is done in some popular educational centres by students. In such educational temples, devotees (i.e., students) are carrying this evil, which is a wonderful illustration of mean-mindedness. What do we anticipate from their likely contribution to society/country in this scenario? There is a strong law against raging. However, students are practicing this wickedness in schools. If they don't regard it, who will do it? Students are considered the future of the country. Thus, the government should enact a good law for outbreaks. There must be a provision in the statute to debar all those involved in this evil from government service, government scholarship, citizenship, voting rights, admission to any other institutions of India for any degree and any other government establishment. Only this hard and fast provision can abolish it. Today the result is that due to it, students are committing suicide or dropping out of education. They are immoral, unsocial, inhumane, and satanic practices; and they are enemies of humanity. Society should not expect anything good from them. I have already suffered from it. Some of my friends have also suffered. However, we were powerless and anyway, we spent four years in college. It is also noted that there are students who do not pay special attention to their studying, but they are interested in conflagration. Many good students suffer. They are kind, and they try to avoid this that cherry but evil students force them to get involved. It is also no infrequent occurrence that a person is killed by them. They are never students, they are cheats on their parents. Indeed, they dig a ditch for our well-established culture."

This news was warmly received by the public. These conceptions of the students of the same college were supported by politicians, social activists, ordinary people, and some students. So, people also raised the demand for its abolition. In the same week, an editorial appeared with the title "Ignorance in the Temple of Knowledge".

This is a farce in that even the House of Learning is an empire of ignorance and evil. Despite being still alive in many, if not most, of the popular educational entities, a great many of the evils of the world have been eradicated. It is truly impressive to find why, if these institutions produce unhealthy and mentally ill individuals in our world, what is going to become of it? What is the future of our country and our society? Several students commit suicide each year because of raging. Some unjust incidents happen in some educational establishments in our country. The government has enacted a bill against it and made it a criminal offence. Notwithstanding all that, it is thriving in certain educational institutions in India. So, the government should pass a strong bill against it for building a new and great India to build a fair society because without a fair society, the future of our country is darkling. Students should also be able to obey the law to destroy it. This evil is against the culture of our society."

This editorial enjoyed an extensive readership and was generally appreciated by the public. So, the government also became very active. Thus, a law was enacted by the parliament to terminate raging. However, Arran kept participating in fiery work though in secret as he was coming into his own. He commented on the review of the media and government for implementing the hardline, strict rule toward the extermination of raging. He said that the government wanted to ruin the personality of the young generation, which they were developing in the educational institutions. Their profound conviction was that to make a country proud, its people should be allowed to experience the difficulties of the contemporary times by teaching them to inflict and be rewarded by, raging as it was building the character of thousands of students per year. According to them, raging was developing an international-level personality.

Chapter - 4

Heavenly Pleasure

The love story of Abby and Arran was unfolding discreetly. No one except Susan knew all this. After passing her examination, Abby was admitted to a post-graduate college in the same city, while Arran was already admitted to a medical college. They studied in different educational institutions, but they used to meet frequently and regularly chatted on *Facebook*. They used to get together, however, their sexual activity was still over the line. They had not yet been sexual but were heading to become sexual, and there was no way in which they would go different ways in their life.

Abby used to go to college and some other boys wanted to win her heart. Arran also considered her activities, however, she has no information about all of this. Arran frequently used to meet her in the college. Sometimes, he suspected her thinking that she had fallen in love with others, so she was not allowing him to have sex with him. But the fact was that she had not fallen in love with any other except him. Arran was determined not to lose sight of Abby at all, and Abby was not in any rush. She was wondering when she should tell her parents about her love.

Suddenly, a new event took place in Abby's life. Some neighbours were going on pilgrimage. Thus, they contacted the parents of Abby and recommended that they make a following. Her parents took it as a good opportunity. So, they expressed their consent and decided to go on a pilgrimage to wash out their sins believing that deities would bless them, and they would be free from sins committed by them in their life. Abby was also interested in going with them. However, her parents recommended that she stay at home to take care of the house. She was docile, so she listened to them and did not go out. They claimed that they would obtain divine favours for her, and she would be blessed to enjoy a happy life for a lifetime, for which she used to pray to the deities all the time.

So she waved them off cheerfully saying, “God may bless you both on your happy journey.”

Her parents said, “Our heartiest blessing for you...”

Blessing Abby they left, and she was left home by herself. But she had no fear of ghosts and thieves. She lived conveniently, and therefore she cooked and ate. She was quite free. Her house was also well-made and very safe. All required materials and equipment were there in her house. Sometimes, her neighbours came and spent some time with her in a discussion. She remained busy doing domestic work. Having left for college she with pleasure announced to her classmates that her parents had recently performed a pilgrimage. So, it was known to most of the students in her circle. Some boys wanted to take advantage of her loneliness. Some wanted to meet her at home to express their love to her, but she did not allow them to do so. They tried to improve their relations with her but in vain. They disclosed their own body language, and their feelings and, in an attempt to demonstrably convey the sincerity and classical nature of their love for Abby, they narrated the process. Having beheld her beauty, their heart became ice and moved towards her. None of this was apparent to Abby, but Abby was very reserved and allowed no one to kiss or hug her. However, they wanted to do so. Thus, they remained colourless and heavy-minded.

They also exchanged some study materials to exchange their love, but there was no impact of all this on Abby and she was adamant that she would not let anyone touch her till the final consideration of what was proper for her.

She said, "No...no..."

She never said, "Yes."

There was an informal competition among boys to win her heart to gain her charming body because they did not know that she had fallen in love with Arran. In contrast, she long suppressed her love secret in her heart.

Thus, she gave back the colour of the love, but inwardly, she also overflowed in love and passion. It was that she was lost in thought as to what was her love for Arran. So, she could not sleep at night and used to think the whole day and night about her love. Each night as she lay in bed, she imagined herself in love with Arran. She became unable to close her eyes while she tried to sleep. Nights passed without sleep. She became restless and left her bed. She tried to control her sexual passions but in vain.

Arran also understood that Abby's parents had already undertaken a pilgrimage and that Abby was residing at home alone. He was certain that the moment of ecstasy had arrived at him. He was determined that he would not leave her untouched in the meantime. He decided to walk up to her, however, he feared that if he did go there, someone would see him. It was no walk in the park to get into her house by night. It was though that he was determined to go to that place to enjoy her physical attractiveness.

He muttered that now he would do or die he would have sex with her that night, or he would cut and throw his private organ. Now it had become quite intolerable for him. Years passed, but he could not enjoy her charming body. Now he could not linger even for a day. His private organ had become as hard as a rod that could pierce a hundred young girls at a time. He was trying to be cool but in vain. Now only Abby could get him cool. All of these conceptions were haunting the mind and the heart of Arran. He had become too restless.

In the meantime, sweat was coming from his body. The impression was that it was a hot day in June when the weather was cool. He was too excited about doing sex acts and wanted to have sex with her then and there. He was on the bed and shifting his side point by point in a restless manner. He was not thus, in a position to control his sexuality. So, he decided to meet her tonight.

It was the month of July – one of the most effective months of the rainy season. Darkness had enveloped the *Earth Mother*. However, in the meantime, night rain poured down unceasingly. It was thundering and lightning. It seemed that heavy rain would embrace the earth and *Lord Indra,* the god of rain, would destroy the earthly drama of loss and gain joy and sorrows...life and death. However, it did not happen and after a few hours, light rain started. In the meantime, Abby was alone and restless because of her extreme desire to have sex with the satisfying one.

Fortunately, during this period of heavy rain, thunder, and lightning Arran came to her bedroom climbing the water pipe of her house. She saw her and welcomed him. His garments were wet, so she said to remove, them but not to change them. He did so and went to bed with Abby.

The heavy rain awarded heavenly pleasure to them. Immediately, they engaged in sexual acts and pleasured each other to the best of their ability. They all agreed not to reveal any relationships with their husband and wife. Hence, they went on with their life journey of love and procured full sex acts by visiting guests' hotels in the city. No one knew about their love affairs, and it was going on secretly.

By contrast, regardless, anyway, or anyhow, for whatever reasons the circumstances might have been or whatever it was that Arran's studies were, in medical school, he passed their medical examination and achieved the highest grade. He was announced champion and received his medal. He secured the degree of Doctor of Medicine. Following the completion of this degree, a new direction in his life began six years later. Now he was filled with pleasure and feelings. He pictured his future and it seemed as if all would be under his own control. He became such a wellspring of hope that he was pushed to take any action, anywhere, anytime in the future. He didn't buy the idea that "the future is bleak, and is a mystery even to all across the world." He stated "as present is transparent, future is perspective."

Some days passed. Experiences of pleasure also reduced, and the strong desire to work to make money embraced him in the way that others did. Thus, he decided to set up a hospital in his hometown. With that idea, he was looking for a grand and beautiful structure in the right place. He found several buildings for it. For one month he would be able to buy up a building for his hospital this way. Without delay, he began hospitals with a message of hope. The city was already a comfortable health facility and when this hospital was opened, there was great satisfaction among people. The name of the hospital was also very impressive Jan Service Hospital. It was inaugurated by the then Health Minister. In the inaugural lecture, he delivered a hi-fi philosophical lecture.

He said that that was a matter of great joy that in this city of Sun God, a new hospital had been founded by a highly qualified and brilliant doctor. Perhaps this was a boon of the Sun God. He further remarked that Arran is the future of the city. There have always been hospitals, but not this kind of hospital. He had enriched the city with modern medical facilities. His work was worthy of kudos, and he had truly made a most virtuous effort. From time to time, the affairs of medical organ theft that took place in some hospitals used to be brought to the media. However, he too was convinced that there would be no issues of this sort in this hospital. (Minimize or avoid the use of the facilities of this modern hospital if deemed necessary). Arran was proud of the city. He, therefore, thanked him.

In fact, the Jan Service Hospital became very famous in a few months only and several patients were admitted there for treatment daily. The signboards of the hospital were placed at various locations within the city. Attention of individuals was intentionally or unintentionally, captured by those signboards. No one could pass any street of the city without seeing its signboards or pamphlets because the walls, crossroads, streets, etc were covered with all this.

Arran had also employed some other doctors in the hospital, and he headed all of them. He remained present there from 10 am to 6 pm and treated about 200 patients daily. There were several members of the medical staff along with several well-maintained bedrooms for patients. All the latest facilities were available there. However, service charges and bed charges are very high but not so like hospitals within metropolitan cities. The poor were provided free-of-cost beds in the general ward, and they had to pay the price of medicines only medicines in colourful and attractive strips or packets. Its outward look was so attractive that patients became very happy, and it seemed that only its look could cure them. Patients were tremendously satisfied with the hospital and its hospitality towards them. Multiple patients from across the country visited the clinic for treatment. It was advertised in newspapers, magazines, and local cinema halls as well as approaching people using the high sound emitting mobile loudspeakers by mimics. Posters were also pasted to bus stops, crossings, pavements, and walls. Most of the roadside walls were covered with posters mentioning every facility available in the hospital. The condition was that any person going to the city with purpose was able to observe or forced to read the posters of the hospital. Observing it, they became ruminative and they debated it. They desired to go to the hospital if they fell ill in the future, and also promised to go there if necessary. They reasoned that the hospital was a place for the average person since its name implied so. However, they felt much sympathy toward it and expected that in any hospital the patients would be cured easily no matter what disease they have. All the medicines stocked in the hospitals were sold at a 10 per cent discount. People said that it was a balm for the poor in that big city, and it was one of the wonders of the age of materialism. Hundreds of patients were admitted and discharged. People had firm faith that any patient in any situation would be cured there. In this way, Arran became one of the most famous doctors in the city within a year. Afterwards, a number of other medical staff were also hired and he started to take over supervision of the hospital.

'The organ is safe, everything is safe'.

In contrast, "the dream of marriage" was stalking the mind and the heart of Arran, just as it does to all of us mortals at the age of marriage. He wished to get married and was looking forward to the right moment. In this way, more than a year passed. However, he did not reveal the secret of the love. On the other hand, some people discussed his marriage as they were unaware of his inner ideas or his decisions.

When Arran settled and began his career as a doctor in his hospital, his parents also told him to accept the nuptial tie. They said that he had finished his education and had begun his job, so he should marry. But Arran advised to wait for a moment and to temporally give him the time to mull over his marriage. It was reported that Arran had had sexual encounters with the lady's medical staff.

Some people also said that he wanted to marry a doctor who was a widow and was already working in his hospital. The same lady doctor, who had killed her husband, who was an honest officer in the state government. She was arrested, spent 2 years in prison, and was shortly released from prison. After her release, her parents told her not to see their faces because they had been defamed and society had taken them out of the caste. Her parents were living in a state of frustration. They said that she had killed her husband who was a gentleman and belonged to a very civilized family because she had sexual relations with some others and her husband used to say not to do this type of immoral work. Her parents also knew about all this, so they didn't let her enter their house. So, she lived alone in a rented quarter, where several lovers used to visit daily. People knew about her character and discussed it frequently. Others also reported that Arran had had sexual intercourse with the widow and wished to marry her, so he did not marry another woman. But his parents did not want their son should marry a murderer like her, who had killed her husband and who had been taken out of her parents' home.

So, they tried to convince him that he should marry without any kind of delay. Some relatives also visited them for his marriage. But he continued to say, 'Wait for some time...Let me live freely...'

Arran's parents were also defamed because people used to say that Arran lived in the hospital with the widow as wife and husband and used to give his income to her and whenever he got some time he enjoyed her privacy. It was a common matter of discussion among the public and the members of the medical staff of his hospitals. Nothing was hidden and sometimes, some members of the staff had also seen him on the same bed and also having sex with the widowed doctor. Others also expressed that this was the single ultimate cause why he had hired her in his hospital; otherwise, she was not appointed to her in any other hospital. She had also started her clinic, but patients didn't go to her clinic and hated her because of her past deeds, the deeds of killing her husband. So, her business fully failed. On the other hand, she could not get any government job because of her criminal record at the police station. However, due to all these reasons, his parents of Arran were pressuring him to marry.

Fortunately, the mystery was disclosed. A miracle came to them. The curtain went out. The sex force came to light. It became active. The waiting period passed. Bliss came to them freely. The matter came to light suddenly when Arran declared that he would marry Abby. The matter of his marriage became public.

On the other hand, Abby's parents also wanted to marry her to any fortunate man, but she said that she had already chosen her life partner, who was Arran. They then approached Arran's parents with the request to unite their daughter (Abby) with one of them in marriage.

When Arran disclosed that he would marry Abby, his parents said that several better proposals had come to him for his marriage, so he should choose one among them. But he refused, flatly saying that he would marry only her, or he would remain unmarried his whole life. Bali, after going to her home to complete a social ritual, did so with a good heart. Both the family were very happy about getting a suitable match. When he came back from there, some of his neighbours asked about the new ongoing relationship, and he replied very happily.

He also reported that they had matched to a very good allele. Their becoming daughter-in-law was highly qualified. She was very charming and seemed like a fairy. They were looking for this kind of proposal and fortunately enough, they got it. She was slim and long. She was so smart. They also said that several proposals of rustics came to us, but they rejected them forehanded.

Abby's parents were also very happy getting a doctor's son-in-law and the richest man in the village. They said that Abby was fortunate she could get a handsome and rich husband. They were also proud of him and told that they regularly prayed for this, so they have each a good quality mate for their daughter Abby who also belonged to his level and was no less than him in any respect. She also belonged to a very rich family in which most of the members were highly qualified and held high government ranks. Every facility was available in her family. They live very luxuriously. She was also a highly qualified woman. It was also known by the people when he decided to marry her. Their marriage was settled and they were betrothed. The date was fixed for this purpose. The preparation for their marriage began, but not according to the customs of the village, but rather in their ways which he considered modern and suitable.

The date based on the programme, Arran's madrigal party arrived at Abby's father's house on the day of the wedding in hundreds of vehicles that were very ornate and it looked as if they were something from heaven. Decorators were called from metropolitan cities. Flowers were purchased from well-known flower traders. The fine perfume was purchased on the internet, and it was spread upon them in such a way that the smell could be sensed by those who were at a distance of several kilometres from the site of the party. There was high-agency management and it looked as if there was a royal romance. The celebration was short-timed but of a high standard. Their relatives, neighbours, friends, and others had been invited according to tradition, and they were highly regarded. The smiles of the guests and hosts, was seen as was seen during the celebration of different rituals related to an arranged marriage. There were no lyrics sung by women except that of young boys and girls who were dancing on the roads with the tone of a disc jockey. There was a brief, hi-fi and professional party for each ceremony just to satisfy formality, and after a couple of hours, all was over. The people had taken wine in high doses. The buffet system was adopted there. Food was prepared by well-established chefs of a crockery house in the city. They were of excellent standard, and they cooked the latest kind of food. The plates were floral and piled high with sweets and veggie "chuck" (i.e., pieces). Various food items were provided, but there was none of the typical fare in their meals. All of them were out of tradition or unused previously, but fully acceptable in modern society. All objects were in some food stalls inside festive tents that looked like brides. How beautiful the tents were, which cannot be said in words, but can be imagined easily knowing that most of the people were unaware of such models, designs, and cuts, and visitors were served by young and smart girls called from metros.

People said, "What is all this? Are these tents or brides? Is this vegetarian or non-vegetarian? Oh! Our mouths ache eating it. How much! Oh! Our eyes ache to see it. Food restriction, all of these circuits are crucial as they influence food intake regulation by assessing calorie intake and providing information on nutrient levels, energy balance, and feeding satiety, in order to determine the optimal amount of food to eat. Aha! Apparently, the stomach is supposed to be stuffed, just to see all this, and we don't need to eat all of this! Aha! What!"

All the food stalls were divided into parts. They were Indian Food Stall, Chinese Food Stalls, European Food Stalls, Arabian Food Stalls, etc. Coffee house centre, tea stall centre, cold drink stall centre, English wine stall centre, Indian wine stall centre, chat centre, ice-cream centre etc. Everything! It appeared that was in a tiny amount, i.e. As they congregated at the celebration of marriage, it appeared that they were beneath the heavenly tree of divine pleasure. They had enough wine, and so, having forgotten all except the fact that they had to sing and dance, left with. However, among them, a few were stripped and nearly naked, but no shyness existed since they were humiliating themselves within the culture of the civilized world. A few men in the city were admiring and urging each other to do so. A portion of them, with either sex, held them on their lap and danced, sang and giggled together. Men and women danced together and embraced one another. The road was blocked, and regular vehicular traffic was prohibited from entering that road. Men embraced women, and women embraced men. The parliament had passed a strong bill that a man could not stand behind a woman even for fourteen seconds and if anyone did so the police would arrest him in connection with the sexual assault. There were so many cases of this type running in the court. However, at least in the meantime, there was no sexual assault and they were open to doing all this. They have reported that one of those moments was complete freedom.

But a wonderful one that if a man was behind a woman only for fourteen minutes though untouched, he could be arrested in connection with the sexual assault, on the other hand, the men and women were embracing one another in objectionable conditions, but acceptable. Even so, there was no complaint, no unhappiness, but a feeling of enjoyment.

When the rituals of marriage were fulfilled, Arran and Abby were tied with the nuptial tie. So, following her marriage and after leaving her parental home, she migrated to her husband's place of residence. Aliens became her relatives, and her family members became aliens. With the finishing of the wedding rituals, the beauty of the home of Lara, who was the mother of Abby, reached Arran's home. Reaching there, some social and religious rituals were fulfilled. But they were also not traditional, but rather modern.

The dowry or presents made to him were enhancing the beauty and riches of his house. They were arranged by him. Those items were a car, washing machine, television, diamond ring, a golden chain, cellular phone, refrigerator, etc. Seeing all this, people discussed their status and affluence, and for it, they held responsible to God and their fate. Days went by, however, the most important topic of conversation was the issue of the current condition and dowry received by Arran. People discussed everything and style and felt pleasure. The non-juristic, pair-wise, matched relatives in-laws of equal relation, controlled for his wifehood night. Everything necessary for them was managed, and they passed the night for which they had been waiting for years. The night was socially acceptable. They availed their right at night. In the meantime, Arran was singing 'Today is the wedding night, I'm unclothing you...And enjoying full-moon pleasure' very lyrically and slowly. He communicated his personal experiences to

Abby, and she also communicated her experience to him. Both were in a pleasant mood. The next day they appeared to be satisfied, due to their strong love. In a playful banter among siblings of equal status, their in-laws of equal status did laugh heartily in their moments of joviality. They also left their home to enjoy the honeymoon period and stayed at multiple five-star hotels in different cities and visited multiple historic temples, museums, zoos, Memorials, educational institutions, cinema halls etc. They mentioned their experiences in their diaries. Items from specific locations were also purchased by them. They also liked outdoor spaces, like fountains, lakes, hills, parks, etc. A week later they returned and started to cohabit with their family. After having returned, they talked it over with their sibling relatives. They also discussed the experiences of their marriage very willingly and began to arrange and count the gift items they had got.

They said that there were many edible items! Hundreds of items! Sweets, chops, wine, coffee, tea, ice cream, etc were sold on unlimited supply. How attractive the tents were! Their garments were as attractive and people continued to look at them without any break. They pried all the items. How pretty the lady dancers were! All sexual positions about the sexual dose they took! Different types of wine were available. People became unable to drink. Their mind and heart were filled with wine. So, they were dancing and singing continuously. How attractive the decoration was! The pedestrians, who were travelling through the passage, also stopped looking at it, once. How the tasty smell was felt! They felt and asked about the smell. Other researchers also went there to investigate its effect on the city or its inhabitants. Spices were antibiotic, antiseptic, anti-allergic, antipyretic, and anti-mortal. The fragrance of the spice could protect them against all sorts of diseases. None would fall ill. No one would suffer. The presence of the spice scent would have a good effect on the atmosphere of the city. It would be a pollution-free city and transformed into immortality.

In this process, they became happy and they passed their marital life. All of them were well and happy with one another. Abby's parents were also very happy and satisfied with them, and they said that they had got a 'gem' and 'musk'. The common people discussed their marriage in their own ways.

They usually said, "...Gem and musk at our hands at our home. We need not go to search for all this."

The Editor of The Social Outlook also went to Arran and talked to her. It was also published in newspapers:

"Are you happy?"

"Yes, I am feeling divine bliss."

"What do you mean by life?"

"Life is full of love and romance."

"Are you satisfied with the love marriage?"

"Yes...yes...yes!"

"But the love marriage does not give the chance to one's relatives to enjoy. The marriage is not for the pleasure of the family but for the parties, bride and groom. They, therefore, need not enjoy wedding rituals."

"When a human couple gets married, his or her relatives get enjoyment in their own way. Only the wedding couple do not like it. There is one important fact that one's life is not limited to one's spouse only, rather it also needs the support of the family, society, etc. There are so many ups and downs in one's life and so many steps which are followed by every man. On rainy days, they cooperate with us. When one is in an arranged marriage, there is maximum chance that he/she will come forth to assist us, but when one is in a love marriage, most relatives do not help, and behave indifferently."

"Who asks them to come forward? We have to live in our own ways. We are free and it is our right to live in our own way."

"We are undoubtedly free to live in our ways. However, as we are social animals, we must conform to society and its organizations. It gives us social security, which is simply a bonus for our life."

"We do not need social security. We have secured ourselves. We have degrees, and we can make money. Money is everything. It protects us. We have already set up our hospital which is filching money and money will continue to bring love, peace and rest."

"We also need social degrees. I don't agree with you. Money cannot produce love, brotherhood, peace, rest, joy, etc. It can never produce all this in our life. We are not alone and we cannot live alone. It is wrong for us to wipe the society and its institutions clean."

"I need not want to know the society. We know the roots of love, brotherhood, peace, rest, joy, etc from where all this is produced."

"Indeed, none can live happily in this society who snatches the social right of one's relatives."

"I know to live happily. We know! We will settle on Mars if necessary. Scientists have, meanwhile, created a multitude of other worlds in which a man could exist. Registration for it is open. For love, each a world and nobody has the right to disturb their world."

And so, months went by, and they lived in peace. He continued to work in his hospital. If he was free from his work in the hospital, he used to spend his time at home with her, and he loved her with every breath of his life. He never hurt her, and sometimes they played together. He never wanted to see her work. She spent her time at home and kept watching the television. Sometimes, she liked to cook some special items despite having several servants at her home. Everything was going well and both were happy.

Chapter - 5

Pleasant and Unpleasant

In this way, some years passed. The situation changed over time. It was as if, rather, time was chasing them, but now they were chasers of time. Their charm decreased. Time passed and their love for each other also fell short.

At the time, they felt the deepest love for each other and habitually used sweet words in their daily life. But over time, they had to fulfil some other responsibilities of the family. In this condition, some minor issues used to become major issues because of the lack of understanding.

As it happens to all in the same way, they also came on the ground of reality. Harsh realities of the world began to embrace them. Now they had no such physical attraction as was in the past. The sexual urge was also not as aggressive as previously. The discussion of the pomp and show and the *hi-fi* management of the wedding programmes also became old, gloomy and irrelevant. The pleasure too and to what degree was sensed and also changed, and so was the sexual romance of the wifehood night forgotten. Promises made by one another became gloom and the family strife took its place. They began to wait for a baby, but she could not give birth while more than two years had passed.

Due to all this, on a day-to-day basis, that chasm widened and the family became accustomed to bickering. The clouds of expectations became gloom. The sense of pleasure began to go away from them. They began to think about the future which seemed dark.

Years passed. Abby did not have a baby, and her mother-in-law Dali became increasingly unhappy with her. Sometimes, she used abusive language. It became intolerable for Abby. Later on, Arran also expressed his dissatisfaction with her. They began to quarrel frequently. Dali was frustrated to such an extent that she refused to even look at (her) face/clothes/anything and when she came into contact with anything or her face, she got dismissed from the school and started to verbally abuse Abby.

Dali noted that there was nothing Abby knew except to rebel and that she was a devotee of Charvaka (as opposed to this Therapeutist, who dared to oppose him). Dali was nothing to her. She was meaningless, and her husband Bali was also zero for her. Now the situation was that she did not respect their son Arran. He was superseded by her...she was a commander of their dear son. She treated him as one of her domestic servants. Five years passed, and she did not give birth to any baby. She lacked maternity aspects. She had no feminine consciousness.

Dali said, "Feminism meant a paragon of virtue. But it was far away from her. Females should have a feeling of love, sympathy, libido, mercy, and so on. But all this was far away from her. Her garments were also out of culture. She did not like to wear lady garments, rather she wore too tight and transparent pantaloons which was a very shortcut. As a result, the parts of her body were easily visible. Their generation used to never wear that kind of clothing. But nowadays all those garments which presented as a modest and humble woman are gone. What was all this? Were those garments or the show of the body? The same was the situation with her food. She never touched even one loaf of homemade bread and she hated it all. She had grown fat. It seemed that she would crush anyone. Arran was fifty-five kilograms, while she was of about one quintal. She liked to take only junk food...fast food. Now she seemed like an elephant. There was no chance that she would give birth to any baby in the future because of her mammoth body. She did not move even her body easily. There were seven maidservants, only one less than eight. They continued to serve her. One took her bath. Others cleaned her purse, garments, shoes, and sandals. They made her up. How did she decorate herself and why? Who would ask her? Who looked at her? Not even a dog could have asked her or looked at her. Could an ass look at her or look at a woman like her, who was huge like an elephant! Within five years, her weight doubled. Yes! Doubled! But her virtues sank? Nothing was in its name! Several bank accounts had crossed the limits of the maximum deposit. A hundred per cent is sinful! Several bank accounts were in her name but on account of virtue feminism, or humanism. She addressed her mother-in-law as an old woman."

Abby said, "O old woman."

Dali remarked that she had never employed such kind of vocabulary for her mother-in-law.

Listening to her, Abby got fired. Telling her insults that she was an old woman and that she should not have said any of this. She warned not to excite her...not to burn her. Dali's language was intolerable for Abby presently. So, she said not to speak; otherwise, the result would be adverse.

After some time, Abby moved towards Dali, but she closed her bedroom inwardly and began to weep for some minutes. Later on, she began to deliver her lecture from her bedroom, because she had no courage to come out of the room, and she was very afraid of Abby.

In the meantime, Dali had closed her door inwardly and Abby was abusing and warning her outwardly. She was also dissatisfied with her fate that she married such a person like Arran and in such a family in which they ate homemade food which was a symbol of their rusticity. She frequently repented of her bad luck and considered herself as a misfortune woman, who possessed everything before marriage and lost everything after marriage. She frequently expressed herself to the family. All these happenings helped them to increase the gap between them.

Bali, who was Abby's husband's father, was quite anxious about the future of his family as well. He was sorry about all the family bickering and there was nothing he had trouble with his son Arran and daughter-in-law Abby. He was not pleased with her role in the family, and he refused to enter her shadow or gaze upon her face at all. He said that Abby frequently used to watch television, so she had gone out of the roots of virtues. He believed he had lost everything in the family because of the strife caused by Abby.

He said very bitterly that then their house had been turned into cinema halls. There was not only one television in the house but rather half a dozen. She kept herself pasted into televisions every hour. She ate while watching television. Televisions were also kept in the bathroom and toilet.

He continued to say there was one other important thing that was the mobile phone for her. Everything was on the mobile.

He said that she had ruined everything about our dynasty and she seemed quite unwell for our family. According to him, she had snatched our peace and rest and she always overlooked them and would not take a cup of tea to them.

But her reaction was harder than that of Bali. She also selected her route for her protest and developed a routine for living with the family as she reported here. In the language of the court, it could be said that there were filings of counters and rejoinders daily. One after another occurred and neighbours enjoyed it happily. Another person also reported that one-act plays by them very often. She abused her in-laws and scolded them. As she got up in the morning, she began to murmur against them. On occasions, she would run after them to strike with her she-shoes and sandals. That is, her in-laws fled out of it and shut down their rooms from the inside. But she knocked on the door forcibly and challenged them to open the door if able to fight against her. She also hurled hard and dense stones against the door to shatter it but did not succeed. When she did so, no one dared to face her, and they said that she was a lioness which could at that time.

In the meantime, Abby was very violent. Loudly she claimed that she was not their maid. She wanted to know. Was she her slave?

Saying, "O dog! O bitch!"

Abby said that her she-shoes and sandals were flowers for them. She reported that she wore the shoes as well as rose flowers for them– she would pet some dogs in their name – and look at their face. What was their look like? Their appearance was reminiscent of either a she-jackal or a bitch, while hers resembled the moon. She was no less brilliant than the famous ancient Greece beauty. She was better than Helen. She said that they had spoiled her life...they had wasted her future. Arran was like a ram, not like Ram. She was, in fact, the only one who did marry him; otherwise, there could not have been anyone who would have.

Further, she said that Arran wasted her virginity and beauty and now she was unable to live long in such a situation to face day-to-day family strife, and she would consume poison. She filed cases against all of them under the *Dowry Act*. According to her, it was indeed a friend of all women. She thanked those who passed this law. They were real well-wishers of women and if the husband failed to award bliss, the *Dowry Act* came to help women. If God failed to grant justice to women, this act awarded justice to them. So, all the women thanked them.

Having all that said, she went toward her bedroom and picked up a packet of poison. When she was about to eat some tablets, her in-laws went to her and dissuaded her from taking them. But she continued to do so for some weeks or some days, and her in-laws continued to soften her in any way.

When they softened her not to do so, she told them, they had known what the Dowry Act was. Now they had its clear-cut knowledge.

She said very seriously, and they said not even a single word. Apparently, they had abandoned her free and without any treaty. The result was that her in-laws remained away from her because they were afraid of the act. They seemed like tired and hopeless soldiers and became lean and thin.

On the other hand, she was active and hopeful; and she was usually challenged to face her if they had the capacity. Although they kept their mouths shut and remained silent, they lacked the fortitude to oppose her. Meanwhile, it seemed that they were her audience and she was their resource person they were listeners, and she was an orator they were devotees, and she was a preacher.

After some days, a new event occurred. It happened to Bali that he was very tired, and had just come from the market. He seemed very nervous and sad. He had lain in a bed in his bedroom murmuring to himself.

The *Dowry Act* had ruined the lives of crores of people as there were so many false cases in the name of the *Dowry Act* in courts. That, unfortunately, had worked for some but not for others. Bali was not immune from this phenomenon either and was concerned that if it were done spoiled families and as a consequence, their children were going to be spoiled as well.

He began to cry, 'alas...the *Dowry Act*! What are you?'

He stated that it was a powerful bridal to the male culture. He regarded it as a powerful commander. He stated that since God did not insist on commanding mankind, it did will to do so effortlessly. He released the prerogative of liberty to women to become anything they want...Right or wrong...Social or unsocial...Moral or immoral. Oh, male-kind! What happened to them? Everything had gone from their hands. They had much to lose and nothing to gain. She-shoes and sandals, however, were at their fingertips now by contemporary women – the children of the modern world. Whatever they may be! They were either gentle or an idiot or characterless or adulteress. In the name of the Dowry Act, they crushed all male-kind. However, in this condition, they were clenched in the hands of women. They commanded them. They ruled over them in its name. But, on the contrary, they were useless. They were hopeless and could be sent to prison. Their legal side was stronger and they were weaker. The court listened to them regarding the law. No one listened to us. She was uncontrollable, like the west wind. She could shoot them and they could be burned easily. She had sucked out nothing in terms of chivalrous and other virtues and had grown up. Therefore, Bali chambered all of it in his room and uttered not a sound to anybody.

Meanwhile, Abby was in the bedroom, literally listening to all this. So, she couldn't tolerate him.

She reached him and beat him with her shoes and sandals, saying, "This is the award to you by the *Dowry Act*. Take it. Accept it. Otherwise, go to jail or hell."

Once she saw it, Dali ran out and locked the room shut to protect herself from the torture of Abby's shoes and sandals.

Subsequently, she only said, "She will fracture my legs and will be turning out my handicap. She is very idiot and heavy as an elephant."

Then it seemed that her lecture was finished. He spoke nothing and Abby went out of his bedroom, he closed the room inwardly so that she could not attack him the second time. Eventually, both Dali and Bali, remained sitting in their rooms. On the other hand, Abby continued to abuse and scold them for hours. She also challenged them to utter even one word to any woman. But both Dali and Bali were silent. She also kept silent and the night passed.

Thus, some days also passed. Nothing was going well or unwell. But the strife was switched off. They did not speak to each other or approach each other.

In this way, some weeks passed. Counters and rejoinders were not witnessed or filed. A bustle was not seen for some days. The neighbour also took a breath of relief. Abby held in deep veneration the Dowry Act and used it in the same manner, but never explicitly. Even a single word was not coming out of their mouths, and it seemed that everything was normal.

About a month passed. Lara came to meet her daughter and her in-laws. Nevertheless, Abby divulged her concerns about her family to her mother and stated an intention to return to her family home.

She aimed to take the opportunity of her being there and instil into their minds and hearts a poisonous substance to easily manage her in-laws at her convenience. So, she said very passionately addressing 'o my respected mama!' according to her, she was bleeding there. She was suffering there. They would kill me. They were beasts and not a single feature of man, at all. They lived like animals and ate like animals. They have eaten home-cooked food and do not like junk food and fast food. They did not like her or her good health. They considered her as a maidservant of the family. Arran was not human but an animal. He did not love her, but he hated her. Was she their servant? Was she not a princess in her mother's house? Would she live there as a maidservant? She said that all this was impossible and impossible! She would not live here. They tortured her unnecessarily. She used to visit the police station and she would lodge a complaint against them under the Dowry Act and they would die in custody. She would not move in there and she would take poison. Thus, she tried hard to convince herself that she was living in a very wrong family and that she was a very gentlewoman.

She asked her mother several questions. She said, "Do you like to see me dead? Am I not your daughter now? Am I not your lovingly? Haven't you created me to be killed here? I will never live here. I can die, but I will not live here."

Lara was listening to her very cautiously and carefully. She gazed into her bedroom and into all of the rooms of the house. She also entertained herself by looking at photographs of movie actors and athletes. TVs were present, five smartphones, and a computer with a broadband connection were in her bedroom. All this was enquired by Lara very deeply.

Seeing all of this, she took her daughter Abby on her lap and a minor child and persuaded her to live happily and harmoniously with her in-laws. She added that all of which could happen to anybody, and that she should become acclimated to living at the level of reality, and not at the level of dreams.

She was mature. So, she understood all this. She said to her to consider the issue seriously. She addressed her saying, 'My darling daughter Abby!' She said to consider it again and again!

She said, "Life is full of problems and challenges, and they continue to come and go, and one continues to pass one's life. So, all must not bend before it. Man must struggle against them and live happily and peacefully. So, she must learn to respect her in-laws. One cannot live alone in this world. As time passes, about the partners involved in the marital relationship/cohabitation, the spouses' attraction reduces but this does not imply that "living together is out of the question". It is one of the parts of conjugal life. So, you must serve her elders to show her human sensation despite several servants in her family. If one serves one's relative, it does not mean that one is a servant. Life is not a thing just about making up stories, watching TV, playing PC games, using mobile phones or using a computer, but all the things need to be done by us, and you should also try to do all the things. You are an educated woman, who can understand everything. Though you see it in newspapers, television and computers, it is not the whole picture. All this is not the whole world. The world is wide and large. Virtues work as chains to connect man to man. Virtues are immortal fruits and are a must for every man. The Dowry Act is not able to bring joy to a person's life, or any other's. No law can provide joy in life. Only man-to-man companionship can give happiness to any human. The Dowry Act has neither soul nor blood...neither mercy nor sympathy. So, it cannot provide happiness in your life. It is helpful for those, who want to gain love in fields who want to grow love in fields, not for those who pass the real life. Not surprisingly, love arises in our cognition. I, therefore, suggest you live here peacefully. This is your own home. After your marriage, we have become your aliens. They are your own."

She knew how to solve anything in a good manner. She was a good mother who brought up her daughter in the path of social and worldly knowledge. Whenever anyone could have succeeded thanks to her ideas, nobody should have failed because of family breakups. However, the state of the world is not yet prepared to let any of us live blissfully and without tension.

She said that there was nothing wrong there. Everything was well. They were good. In the family, there was no issue and she could happily and serenely live. Arran was besides a great guy, and precious, like Abby. He was her heartbeat, like her. Both were equal to her. Her in-laws were also very gentle. She suggested she remain far away from the clouds of doubts. Everything was crystal-like and clear. So, her future was resplendent there. What was not in her family? Everything was in her family. All this way to pacify her was wonderful.

Saying all this, she pacified her to live there, and she became ready to do so. She became soft, and outwardly it seemed that there was nothing wrong there.

She said calmly but seriously that if she said to live there, she was ready to live, but one day she would find her dead. She would lose her. She would not live in this world. She appeared different, for example, like her in-laws. Abby said that she had no love for her. It seemed that she was not her daughter.

She asked her mother, "Why have you given birth to me? Only to kill me? Yes! I am sure! You want to kill me."

However, Lara was all calm and still and did not oppose it. She tried to convince her.

She said that Abby was undoubtedly her own. Arran was also her own, like Abby. Both were her own. Both were equal to her. Everything would be good. Prepare the ground for love, peace, and rest. Forget the past of family strife."

"OK…," said Abby very slowly.

Lara prayed over Arran and Abby and gave homage to Arran's parents. Nothing was on record in terms of ill-will or discrimination towards her in-laws. She was happy and satisfied with the family. On the same day, she departed from there smilingly, and then there was no sign of family strife, and they were happy.

Chapter - 6

Thunder and Lightning

Arran and Abby were living happily. Having them blessed, Lara returned to her abode. In-laws Abby were absolutely happy with the action Lara had done for peace in their life. They exhaled with a sigh of relief and only felt the best of feelings. Upon that, there was peace and quiet in the family, and that peace was followed by no sight of any rays of family discord. Everything was passing on peacefully.

Arran visited the hospital at the scheduled time and was properly observed. He was also quite relieved the volcano had gone cold and, as such, would be able to live in bliss and peace. He moved into his house as a man who had no problem and if it would come that would be solved automatically as had been then solved. He felt that all was well and failed to understand the plan of his wife which was inwardly going on.

They were living happily. They wanted to go on tour to secure the blessing of deities for peace, rest, and affluence of the family. After a few days, they both embarked on a tour and toured a variety of sites of religious and historical interest. However, this behaviour was completely transformed when they went to the temple of Lord Krishna in Mathura. They admired the classical love between Radha and Krishna. In the interim, they also witnessed the undying affection of Sita for Ram and of Savitri for Satyavan. They also promised to live happily and peacefully. They enjoyed the spiritual beauty of the temple and promised to employ the spiritual affinity in their life too.

After a week spent in the same way, they returned home and they looked changed, which was quite apparent to the members of their family and neighbours. On returning home from their travel, they purchased some memorabilia for the location where they travelled. These were offered to their family members, happily. They began to talk with one another. She respected her in-laws, and they also brought something to her from the local market, she accepted all this and expressed happiness to them.

Now everything seemed changed. Negative ideas changed into positive thinking. Nothing abnormal in the family was readily observed. Neighbours were also astonished, seeing their condition. They assured them that family peace was only temporary, that they were storing energy for a later battle, and were clearing the battlefield for the fight to come.

In this way, about three months passed. Everything was going well. A sense of peace and rest was following them. However, one day, Bali was upset with Dali for a couple of petty grievances, and Dali was getting angry at her. In the meantime, Abby was in her bed-chamber, and hearing his fury, she went to him and said to him that he was talking at her and of Dali. Yet, he told her that he was any statement made, not for Dali, but for Abby. However, she did not know the point and went mad. Her face also turned fiery. Later on, she began to abuse him and also challenged him to come out of his bedroom. In the meantime, there was a strong wooden rod in her hand and she was holding it offensively.

At the same time, Bali was surprised to receive such an attitude from Abby and told that the belonged to yelling at Dali and not at her. However, she was unwilling to listen to him anything longer and continued to mistreat him by claiming that he had maltreated her. Getting the abnormal behaviour of Abby, he got fired. He could not tolerate the behaviour of his daughter-in-law.

He said that Abby had gone mad. He was scolding Dali. He was not chastising Abby and she was by no means lovingly abusing him.

He said, "The television had made her mad. It wasted the whole civilization. It spoiled our culture and sacrament. Alas, television! It was the greatest enemy of mankind. It brought Western civilization to our country. He had ruined Indian philosophy the philosophy of the *Gita* and the *Ramayana.* All live in its empire. Our houses had been turned into cinema halls, and they lived in it slept in it and ate in it. One could easily imagine the situation of society and our lives because of television only, which has ruined their culture. But now she was quite unable to tolerate it. It had got Abby out of root. Just now, she would destroy the root of Abby's evils."

Saying all this, he entered the room television and took the television in his hands he threw it on the main road. Yes! On the main road, he brought the whole family to the main road. Throwing it, he barricaded himself in a room for his protection. With that knowledge, people gathered and started to debate the problem in various ways. They knew the detailed account of the issue and its result was that the family was defamed. They continued debating it over the following days, and it was a topical point of discussion on every street in the city.

On the other hand, there was a tussle between Dali and Abby. Bali was struck by Abby, but he was unscathed since he had already shut his bedroom externally to the world. Dali was unable to seal off her room, and she was violently attacked, and severely beaten. She also beat her. Both were injured lightly. Several domestic items were destroyed. Arran also kicked Abby and went to the hospital. He spent a short time so as not to watch family drama more distant. The following day some newspapers reported this news, which people read with interest. They discussed, viewed, and reviewed it in their own way. This golden chance to read a piece of news related to the high profile family came to them. They knew about the internal issues of the family. They also discussed their past and present. This was a good family film and better than all the other romantic films done by their neighbours which they happily consumed.

Abby's parents also read the news regarding it. Reading it, they got fired and dealt with it as a crime against their daughter. So, they both went to her house, and some of her relations accompanied her and started to harass her in-laws. They fought them for killing too but some neighbours protested, and the issue improved smoothly. Then a case meeting took place, and the case was debated. Their arbitrators essayed to soothe each side and induced them to carry on together happily and uncomplainingly. However, her parents were stressed, and they were not listening to their "rebuttals," and she was talking like it was the fountain that used its effervescence to make her pronouncements. Doran, the father of Abby, was too annoyed with them and wanted to shoot her in-laws. He was speaking loudly.

He stated that she was a very special woman, and very humble like Sita. They never even spoke a word of disapproval towards her, yet they were butchers ready to kill her. They had never beaten her or scolded her. She was their darling. She was their heartbeat. Was Abby their subject? Why did they want to rule over her? They were not her ruler. They had not produced her, but they had each done so. She was neither their subject nor their servant. They always wanted, to that, to not see their daughter crying, or working. She would not obey them, rather they might obey her because they had taken the hard currencies as dowry, and they had given them as per their mouth demand. They were poor previously. They could weigh all of them using hard paper money. They could also weigh their house. They warned them that they did not recognise them. They would be sent to hell.

They asked them many questions. "Do they want to go? Did you hear the name of the *Dowry Act*? Do you know it? Do you want to know? Tell me. The police will come soon. Every one of you will spend a good part of your life in prison, and you will die in prison. It will become your home – your patent home. The government constructed this patent home for the kind of people like you. Idiot! Being an idiot in Sun God City is no laughing matter. We are His devotees and He is with us. You will ruin yourself. Do you want to be ruined? Why do you torture my daughter Abby? Why?"

Arran's parents were not equipped to manage all of this and were also angry at her and her parents. They all too readily repented of the union of their son with Abby. However, they appeared helpless and their response was developing very slowly in their heart and mind due to the tenacious clutch of the *Dowry Act*. They knew that there were thousands of people in jail because of the false cases filed in different police stations and courts under this act. "That is they lacked the courage to act violently like their parents, Abby's parents, etc. Their reactions were slow but bitter. Some people said that their ideas were considerable.

Dali spoke in a very quiet way that they were the messengers from the inferno and their daughter was a physical demon. She said that her mother was a witch and Abby was the grandmother of witches. She would swallow them. They would be chewed and digested. Since she arrived at their own family, they were consumed by an ocean of woes, and they were helplessly soaking in it. They were quite helpless at her hands. They gave birth, not to a woman, but rather to a black demon, and all they could just imagine. Yes, she said that it was unrealistic anyone could survive by living with a hellish Abby since that was very difficult. They had agreed to escape from her and promised to get their daughter back, to be able to breathe freely. Their breath had been blocked. Day-to-day strife! Their son had turned black because of it. They said that they would not let her live here. She had taken out their soul. She never regarded them or never listened to them. She did not know even a way of courtesy. It was meaningless for her. Fashion was her everything. Making up! Decorating her body, not her soul! Appearances suggested that she would have to play a role in a fashion walk or a beauty pageant. Every fashionable item was used by her, and she had everything except virtues. They refused to condition her to live there.

They said, "We are not in a situation to tolerate her now. O, people! Let us breathe! Save our lives! Save us! We are dying. Our life has been turned into hell. It is very clearly observable, and aside from us, no one else has directly observed it. Whoever wants to see hell, must come to our place. O God, save us! Take us out of hell. Twenty-four hours for television, of television, and by television. She tells us she has not flipped a spoon in her own home. Which type of sacrament, she possesses? To which sacrament has she been raised?

Who has given birth to such a powerful witch who can move this tender earth? She can swallow the whole earth."

In the meantime, Arran and Abby were listening to her separately, and they were quite silent not because they wanted to remain silent but rather because arbitrators were convincing them not to react.

After some time, both were called by them. Hence, Abby came to them. In the meantime, she was weeping bitterly. They asked her about her situation in the family. However, she did not utter a single sound but cried. They tried to pacify her but in vain. If they couldn't, they told her she was a naturally humble woman who had fallen victim to the malice of her husband's family. Her parents said that only because of her coyness, which was one of the qualities of an Indian Hindu woman, she was not speaking any words. They said that she had been tortured by her in-laws.

According to them, her in-laws had spoiled her life. According to one arbitrator, he has not met such a righteous woman in his lifetime. He reported (her) to be as soft as Sita and trapped by the cruel fist of Arran and her husband's in-laws i.e., the villainy of Arran's in-laws driving her into Arran's grasp and so had to be bundled up in legal cells or to hell. He also stated that she required a kind husband but unfortunately, fate had brought her to such a terrible circumstance, and so she had absolutely nothing to say.

But when Arran listened to 'a single word', he got fired and his face turned red. So, he came to him and said that he did not know her.

He explained that Abby was not a voiceless figure, but a spherical pyre of flames ready to consume the world. She could burn all the oceans of the world. She was a volcano who'd ruined it for himself and his family. She knew nothing. 24th-inch television was her whole world. Everything was in it. She was corrupt. She was hot, and she had slept with several men and continued to do so now. She talked over the phone with her lovers. She did not know them. She lived in the market till late at night and spent time in clubs. What was done by her? Only she knew. He did not know. He said he was nothing for her, and she was his enemy no. 1.

Thus, Arran expressed his dissatisfaction and many questions. "Is she my wife who does not love me and follow my orders? She respects the advertisements shown on television. Several mobile phones are her darlings. I have no idea how it is used 24 hours a day. I do not know who contacted her. I ask her about this, but she scolds me. They are her lovers. She rarely lets me touch. You can imagine, how can I live with her? She regards me as a toy and she does not, in any sense, know the sacrament. No morality! No virtues!"

He said that Abby was an evil store, which had made her the mother of fiends. She was a woman of a mind that did not adapt to a single place. But her belonging was in the sky and her feet were in the sky. She lived in the world of fancies. There was no issue until now. She was a barren woman. She was strong nitric acid she could ruin anything on this planet.

In the meantime, she was also subject to the imposition of parents' regulations and dozens of arbitrators' decisions. She was listening to him and boiling inwardly. At times, she held her sandals in her hand to throw on him. But they were assuming her not doing so. So, she was sitting as a gentlewoman, and it seemed that she was a virtuous woman.

Despite their control over her, when she listened to 'She is a barren woman', she went out of their control, and she began to deliver her ideas, not in prose but rather in a female blank verse like an angry poetess.

"O dog! Do you know me? Do you know my parents? We will lick you as jelly and will digest. We'll roast you alive, and no one will come out (to free) you. You consider me as 'nitric acid'. You must know that I am 'super nitric acid plus' which will melt not only your body rather also your soul. I am no more prepared to come back and I know I can go forward only. It is no secret that I am not a typical Hindu woman, but an ultra-modern Indian Hindu woman, who has been shaped by the television and as a product of Westernization. They are my parents – they are my rulers. Do not expect to get me back. I cannot live with you because you are a corrupt man. Your parents are also corrupt. You have several wives. I am not the only one not the only, my wife. You have undergone several women. What are you for me? You are nothing! I will ruin you with my fist. O fifty-five-kilogram puppet! I am over a hundred! Do not compel me to lose my patience! Otherwise, the result will be too adverse. Are you mute? Are you listening to me? Do you understand all this? Are you deaf or mute? I'll spoil you. You must know, that I will never serve you or regard you. You are indeed my servant because my parents have bought...you have been bought by them in the market of matrimony. Your parents have sold you to my parents' hands. You are, however, my attendant and are required to hear anything I may say or order. Who says that wife and husband are equal? The truth is that women are the same as men, and men are the same as women. A woman is a symbol of the Creation and a man is the symbol of a watchman who has to watch over the Creation. Just I am to live with my parents, not with you. As I came to your life, tears entered my life. Woes embraced me fully. Now, how can I live with you? You are not on my waiting list and never will be. I will send all of you to jail and in the future to hell. Just now I am going to the police station accompanied by my parents. The Dowry Act will catch 'one' in the cell and the inferno."

Saying all this, she began to weep bitterly.

Having learned that she will report to the police station, Dali starts to drum and beat on her chest like a drum and also cries herself. She went into zero hours. She became restless, thinking that she and other members of her family would be arrested. She found herself on the ground of woes.

He stated that Abby was not mute, but a globe of fire that could burn the earth. She could burn all the oceans of the world.

He said, "She was a volcano who had ruined his life and his whole family. She knew nothing. 24th-inch television was her whole world. Everything was in it. She was corrupt. Sex was attractive to her, and multiple men, at least, and still she enjoys them. She talked over the phone with her lovers. She did not know them. She lived in the market till late at night and spent time in clubs. What was done by her? Only she knew. He did not know. He said that he was nothing for her, and she was his enemy no. 1."

When Dali knew that she would go to the police station, she began to beat her chest like a drum and began to weep too. She went into zero hours. She became restless, thinking that she and other members of her family would be arrested. She found herself on the ground of woes.

Despite all this, the arbitrators continued their attempts to pacify them and supported their ideas mentioned above. Firstly, they tried to pacify their parents. But they ignored it flatly. After that, they tried to appease them again, for the sake of religion, duty, society and sacrament. They kept doing this for 8 hours for 8 straight hours, in an inn in the city. Even with a lot of toil and hours, however, they were successful and settled. Getting success in their first step, they became happy. They, therefore, moved towards the second step and began to pacify Arran and Abby. But Abby refused flatly to live with him.

Soon, her parents started to break her down and told her that nobody would remarry her because of her bad image. After their hard toil, she was softened and became ready to live with him. But that was not the final solution because Arran was not ready to continue the journey of marriage to her, and he said that she was fully unable to give birth to any baby. Expressions of desire to marry another woman, up to the point of seeking a civil and legal annulment from the matrimonial court. He was not listening to them anything and was thundering like clouds against her and her parents. At the same time, one would think that he would gulp up nature itself.

Arran was very unhappy, and she said that Abby was sterile she was corrupt. Her parents were an idiot. She was mean, and her parents were also mean. They belonged to a mean dynasty of his caste. He was a fine section of our ensemble. Their lineage was meaner than his. He said that he was the greatest among his caste in the village. So, he could live with her. He would like to die but never wanted to spend the rest part of his life with her. It was impossible. He did whatever he said. He said that he never looked back. He never changed his views and decisions. This was the key feature of his family and ancestry. They were well-known persons of the caste and community in the city. The whole city knew it. But no one knew about Abby's family. He reported that only dogs and pigs knew Abby and her parents.

The discussion was going on. They were producing hot words against one another. Nevertheless, the arbitrators of both sides wanted to compromise in the dispute at all costs. They, therefore, continued to soften them, but in vain. Afterwards, an elderly person, who was sitting in the corner, went over to Arran. He told him, to find out the real sense of life. He said that he should not hurt the will of several persons present there. By continuing to do so, he would not gain anything but pain and suffering. He told them he was an experienced man and that they should trust their advice. So, he became ready to do so.

Having heard your opinion, Arran smiled and said, "I accept your decision just as does a man of a hundred years. If you declare, I'm willing to offer her one opportunity to live with me. If once more she retraces the past, then there will be no space for her in my heart and mind. This is my final decision."

In this way, both were pacified to continue their relationship to fame the institution of marriage. Following this, the meeting ended in a comical fashion. Individuals who were present at that site were surprised to see such a stance. Some people said that the comedy was momentary. Their parents have recommended they make a pilgrimage to request God's blessing first. So, they decided to do so.

Chapter - 7

Peace before War

After their compromise, they went to their home. Her parents also visited together and a love party was organized by Bali. They exhaled with a sigh and there was a feeling of calm and relaxation, throughout the family. Everything was going well. It appeared as if they had lost sight of the thunder and lightning of family discord. It was considered inwardly and outwardly. The problem of road TV was forgotten, and peace was followed by the rest. People said that there was an all-around change in their hearts and minds, and the change was a wonder. They said that the mutual understanding saved the family, otherwise there would be something wrong.

They went to a few religious places together, namely, Maihar, Kashi and Vaishno Devi, after meeting. To begin with, they went to Maihar and offered prayers to the Goddess of Strength joyfully and devoutly. They prayed for peace and rest in their life. One week passed by them there, and during this period they visited several other places of Maihar and witnessed the spiritual beauty. They also bought some of the things of the place along with a picture of Goddess Sharda. They enjoyed the spiritual beauty of the temple.

After Maihar, they directly visited Vaishno Devi. Having got the blessing of the goddess, they were overwhelmed by feeling the magical power of the goddess as they felt and expressed it after coming back to their home. They said that when they were praying to the Goddess, suddenly their mouths had been filled with sweetness, which symbolized that there would be sweetness in their life. Performing a return, they also purchased a good number of religious items instead of feminine goods there and their purpose, bags were full of them. During their journey, their attention was never focused on the shops where fashionable items were sold, rather they looked at and into the items which were related to Hinduism.

Finally, they travelled to Kashi and the historic Baba Vishwanath temple and prayed for peace and rest in their life. When they were returning from there they were happy, and their happiness was easily felt even in their luggage which was full of religious items. They took part in a multitude of religious activities that were organised along the river Ganges, the holiest of all rivers. They liked enough the candle worshipping of the river in the evening. They said that their eyes were fixed during it without any kind of rest in it. They particularly liked the spiritual attractiveness and personal feeling of the city. On occasion, they pictured never returning to their native place and living out their days permanently in Kashi.

In contrast, the family members were also very joyful when they stayed home and were eagerly looking forward to their happy return. Some days later they returned to their home and were greeted with love by their family members. Some people said that that was an unusual journey that was performed to replace their honeymoon journey. They respected them after coming back. Arran's parents were also overjoyed and blessed them with their tranquillity. Dali was over-happy and seemed fully changed. Her happiness was uncontrollable, and she narrated it wherever she went.

Dali said very happily to them, addressing 'o my dear! Oh, my heartbeats! Now no one will harm you.'

She reported that they would not get sick as they had the deity's blessing in advance. This was well for them that they had gone on pilgrimage at a young age, while most of the people went on a pilgrimage in their old age. This was 'well plus' for both of them. It meant to say that they had done everything at a young age while others did in their old age, and some of them failed to do so even in their old age. She said that one mistake had been committed, that a widow had touched Abby during the marriage. So, she suffered. Now they had been blessed by deities, hence they would protect them and nothing unwell would take place in their life.

She continued to say that 'Time is omnipotent' it was against us they, therefore, suffered enough in the past but let it go forget the past of woes and sorrows - learn to live in present and wait for a resplendent future. Now they had learned to love and respect elders. They had also learned to pay courtesy. As long as they kept all of this, nothing would go wrong with their life. No problem! She said! They said! Our parents had told us. They did so and waited for all this. Now they do so and would do so, undoubtedly. She expected...they expected. And all deities and spirits had awakened to perceive them. They were in their heart having consumed their sacred food. Their holy food could make anyone problem-free. Now they were quite free from problems. I believed they had already started a new life and her sincerest wish was that for them. All this was communicated to comfort them and make them feel better.

Dali had firm faith and blind belief that the vehicles of happiness would continue to go in the right way. Arran and Abby were also living very happily. They had arranged their house in a new way. Replacements of stills of film stars and athletes were made by stills of gods and goddesses. They were set on the walls in a separate prayer room that already existed in the house. Both of them worshipped daily. But someone said that they whispered, not worshipped. However, these members of the family also acted in this way and also prayed alongside the family. The voice of the shell was audible by all their neighbours in the morning and at night. Its voice took the place of family strife, along with the shoes and sandals. The prayer took the place of abuse. In a week, there was a special religious programme in the family, at least. They distributed holy food after the celebration. As part of the programme, loud religious tunes were played generally and high sound-producing loudspeakers were operated by them. There was an atmosphere of religious programmes in their neighbour.

There was an echo in the house, with a magical quality that could release anybody from sin or evil sense. As if deities had invaded their home, the neighbours were in the sway of an enchantress. The magical atmosphere was seen in the whole family. "That was wonderstruck" was the topic of discussion among members of the populace. The neighbours also joined in sharing the blessed food and experience delighting in it. They thought that the family was the only one who returned from the cusp of annihilation, and this was only made possible with the grace of the gods.

The echo of bell and shell, not only, changed the atmosphere of the family and neighbours rather also the garments of Abby. Her jeans pantaloon and shirt, bra-cut chemise and frock, sex-cut chemise, etc were replaced by the traditional sari and blouse. The sari and the blouse became her craze garments, undoubtedly, and Dali was very happy with her stand. Therefore, she started to name her, "my sweet daughter." She started to tell how her daughter-in-law was a Hindu and Indian sacramental woman, being a lady of virtue and good morals.

Once, Dali was so emotional and unable to control her emotions. She rang Abby and instructed her to sit next to her. So, she sat near her and Dali patted her.

She said, patting her, that Abby was her lovingly! She said to sit on her lap. She was then her heartbeat. Right, she was her lighthouse – the light of her dwelling. So, she was a lighthouse of her family. How virtuous she was! How moralistic she was! She was, really, a paragon of virtues. She had all the qualities of a Hindu woman. Her body shined like a polar star. Upon seeing her, a vision appeared to her. Wherever she was, there was light; wherever light was, there was she. Happiness came with them. Indeed, her presence was the presence of a goddess. She was a goddess. The goddess of her house! She started with 'o Goddess Abby' and Dali could not live without her.

Listening to Dali, Abby became very emotional and began to respect her using polished words. So, she searched for new words in the dictionary to regard Dali. Its result was that Dali's feet moved fast, and she began to weave the threads of happiness in the family, and Abby continued to use sugar-coated words for her mother-in-law.

Abby told Dali was good and that she liked her mom very much. One could rarely find a virtuous mother like Dali. She was a creation. She was the earth. She was her reverend – her goddess. Hence, Abby expressed her sugar-coated thoughts in the form of dictionary words.

These ethereal expressions took their toll on Dali, and she completely lost herself to the past of a family feud. On the other hand, Abby religiously continued to improve her habits at a cognitive level. Sometimes, she used to wear handmade coarse cotton garments and moved into her house as a pet. Looking at her, Dali claimed she was one of the disciples of Mahatma Gandhi. People are astonished knowing all this. Dali was just so taken it was not possible to hide her store of ideas at the cost of Abby.

She said to her that she was not a daughter of Doran and Lara, but rather of the philosophy of Mahatma Gandhi. How Gandhist she is! How much Indianness she had! She was a true supporter of homemade items. However, the moment she became an advocate of multinational companies or American companies. She suggested that she should establish a political party and should initiate a 'home-made' movement, similar to Swami Ramdev, because, she was also one of the pioneers - her work was one of the classics. Lately, her physical attractiveness lay hidden in the fabrics and, hence, her internal organs were very clearly visible thanks to the net-cut blouse; the contours and dimensions of her body were easy to deduce. Dali disapproved of it all, but she ignored it. Fortunately, now she had herself understood everything. Indeed, it was a discovery, and Dali was trying to exploit all this for the benefit of the family. However, she was not informed about the future treatment of time.

She also reported that they had to stay in India. They have to absorb Indian culture and they have to not forget that their culture has a root and if it is ruined, nothing can be saved other than that. An Indian woman was considered a goddess, hence they must try to maintain themselves as a goddess as it was possible in this world, which was full of miseries and problems. They had a very rich culture and traditions. Unfortunately, they were heading in the opposite direction of their culture and were adopting the Western culture which was self-destructive and fatal. Its result was that a good many Indian fortunes were broken every year. Dali proposed to do whatever it takes to be happy but not compromise for virtues. To hurt anyone was an unpardonable sin. They should also consider the notion of sin and virtue. That was the opinion of Dali to lead her to the centre track.

In the meantime, Abby was nodding as 'a devotee nods and realizes to her or his religious preacher'. She understood all that her mother-in-law said and made an apology to Dali. She was happy and satisfied, so she was left to advance as far as was reasonable for her. At the same time, she understood that Indian culture is the richest and the greatest in the world. She believed that the Indian culture commanded mankind to do right and showed a bright path to living happily and peacefully. According to her, the Indian culture provided rights for life.

There was a changed perspective in her life and she altered herself as much as she could. She continued to behave well towards everyone, and she was very cautious about her behaviour and did not think about her looks. She spoke very politely. Individuals were amazed to observe such an alteration in her behaviour. All this was easily felt by anyone. Once, she was for the thunder and lightning once she was known for family strife, but all this became a thing of the past. She was for love and respect. They said that it was only made possible by the change in her heart. Their reaction to her posting was that her behaviour was the outcome of a sudden transformation", for instance. So, people discussed her understanding and suggested others learn a lesson in 'how to change'. Her change was adaptable, and they believed that she was an 'example' she was the ideal in the city and people should imitate her ideals and behaviours. They suggested others follow her, and her footsteps.

Consequently, months went by, and they were having a good life together. No strife. No tussle. No use of shoes and sandals. Love and serenity of home prevailed throughout the family. The dust of the house also knew that then there was no place for evils.

Three months went by and no one in the family got sick. They lived happily and dealt with family issues jointly. There was no evidence of any previous family discord, and they had long since put it aside. Likewise, their neighbours were also taken aback to see such a jovial atmosphere. They said that that was a miracle that they went happily about their lives, no longer remembering the past of noise and violence. They took it as a wonderful one.

They say that man goes along with time, however, some men in wealth think and err that time goes by them. The same happened to Arran and Abby. It seemed that time was following them previously. But currently, they began to follow time. Suddenly, a new thing happened to the family. Some guests had visited there. So several edible items were cooked, and its smell reached the nose of Dali, but food could not reach her mouth. It occurred that sweet food was not served to her because it had already been served completely to the relatives. So, there was no sweet food in the kitchen. Whenever a plate of food was put in front of her, it was not there on her plate. Seeing it, she became angry and threw the dish on the court and began to abuse Abby. A part of the hot ingredients in the dish also reached Abby's body, she was slightly injured. Dali mentioned that the sweet food was eaten by Abby in the kitchen secretly, so Dali did not get any sweet food to eat. She regarded it as her disregard and partiality toward her and said that it was against the Indian culture. However, the reality was that Abby had not eaten it either and she said to her quite politely and flatly about it. She also stated sweet food had been previously consumed by the guests and that she and her husband had not consumed any. But Dali was not ready to believe her.

Both of them delivered their ideas in their own ways. She endeavoured to persuade Dali that the sweet food did not exist and, therefore, could not be served. But Dali did not agree with her and the tussle began between them. Dali continued to abuse her. It became intolerable for Abby. She then went to the police station and filed a report of her family troubles. The police were taken to their house, and they were detained. They were taken to the police station and placed in a jail cell. The matter of sweet food reached the police station. Its aroma was experienced and appreciated by all people walking along the road. The problem led them to the street in front of the house.

It was, however, a novel idea in the history of the city. The general public looked surprised at the fact that they were detained, not as treatment or punishment, but since they were upper-status born lower-status treated people. Its result was that they got fired. When they arrived at the police station, they started to shout slogans to get them out of prison.

"Police administration!"

"Alas!"

"Bali and Dali!"

"Long live."

"Police atrocity."

"End up."

"We will die."

"Or we'll dry."

"Take rupees as you say."

"But release them."

These slogans were hanging overhead, a recipe for agitation of such magnitude that it turned off the police's desire to listen. However, the police were trying to ameliorate them. Even with their strenuous effort to wean them off those chants, they kept chanting slogans and attacked the police station. They also tried to release them forcibly. On the other side, the police tried to restrain them, in vain. Thus, there was police intervention to clear the crowd. They also used a tear bomb. They were caned. Many people were arrested and sent to jail. Some people were injured and sent to the hospital. Some people were killed too. The whole city drowned in deep distress. After death, they were handed over to their families. On the same day, several funeral marches were practiced and the bodies were incinerated in various outdoor crematoria located throughout the city. As if something from the street did rejoice in the event, it appeared that even a lifeless object in the city was excited by it.

On the other hand, Doran and Lara found Abby and placated her to make a deal to solve the case to escape additional trouble. Indeed, both sides readily accepted it and conceded concerning the problem. Thus, since there was no written complaint, they were let go from the police station. However, instead, they experienced remorse and repented of all the dead people in the town solely because of them. Embarrassed they made a compromise and started to live together. The matter was diverted. They said that they were not responsible for any kind of injury or attacking the police station because they had not excited anyone, and they had done nothing against anyone indeed they had been lodged in the prison cell, and no person was in their contact and the police had failed to control the mob.

Both Arran and Abby were living together, but there was a bloodstain in the family and the city. Roadside in the city it was clearly visible. Joy changed into sorrow. Happiness in the past and sorrow at the last! There was an all-around bustle. People discussed it widely and said that Abby was unwell for the city because only because of her there was a loss of lives in the city. Such a type of massacre was never witnessed in the past, as the people said.

People of the city fell into the ocean of distress and repented of such a step taken by them and the action of the police against them. They reported police had unnecessarily shot and killed a great many people. However, the police reported that there was only one way, that they had to shoot at them to control the unruly masses and dissipate them because they had attacked the police station doors and wall and had kitted off some rifles. People said that the government should take necessary actions against the policemen, and they should be dismissed from their service. They claimed the sum of twenty-five lakh rupees as compensation and the government job of the victim's close relatives. Yet, the government has announced a compensation of only two lakh rupees to each deceased victim's family and two thousand rupees to each injured individual, and the family members' government job was not announced.

The people were not satisfied with the announcement of the government. They, therefore, held a social meeting in Ambedkar Park. Thousands of people assembled there. They began to discuss the issue peacefully. They blamed the government for having done the issue not sympathetically. They prepared a memorandum for the same submission to the District Magistrate. Local authorities greatly spoke on the stage and were softly commented upon. None was agitated there, and they decided to mount pressure on the government in a democratic way for the fulfilment of their demands. Singling out the Satyagraha way that has been the mainstay of practicing by Mahatma Gandhi throughout his life for the purpose and constituted a team of eleven persons to continue, they engaged in a strenuous fight. Certain members of the team were connected to certain political parties and they wished to make bread on the matter, consequently, it was not noted by the general population. They failed to understand their inner will, and they expressed their firm faith and full support to them. But then the team prepared another heavy, attractive memo, secretly, later. It was unknown to the common people. Lost, it was, and the doctor put before the District Magistrate.

On the other hand, people were very happy and hopeful about the fulfilment of their demands as some political leaders were also supporting them, and we're sharing their woes and sorrows. One person, who was present in the meeting, was over sure. He was extremely pleased with them and saw them as their way finders.

He said very firmly they were a hundred per cent sure. Sometimes, a thousand per cent sure! They knew that the government would have to listen to their demands to fulfil their demands at any cost because some political leaders were supporting them; otherwise, they were ready to do anything. Anything! They would not go back. It wasn't a job that any of them would have ever considered again. They announced they would continue and establish a core committee. It could have been to its advantage and could have provided responses to their needs. Government would have to give way in order to meet demands, and would therefore have to comply with them. Consequently, they strongly assumed that they would achieve their goal.

People were waiting for the fulfilment of their demands.

In contrast, Arran and Abby were cohabiting. Some reported crying "inwardly" under the same roof, in the same room. It then became clear that they were a long distance from war. But they were undoubtedly passing their lives as the clock continued to tickle even in the winter season or in the summer season. The tickling was obvious to neighbours to feel and sight. "Lovely" was not used by Dali to refer to "Abby" but instead she used to refer to "Unwell" Abby. 'Abby' changed into 'unwell Abby'. Arran also referred to her as 'Unwell Abby' and not 'my love' as was mentioned earlier. They did not ever speak to each other and they appeared as the unmixed chalk from cheese. They got inside as the wind rushed from the west, whatever destroyed or could destroy could blow anything or somebody. They lived together but used a minimum of words for the maximum of ideas in their daily routine. Sometimes, they behaved as mute people. But their activities were usual. On other occasions, Abby also prepared food, and, without a word or sound, provided them. Sometimes, it seemed that they were wordless machines, but their life was going on.

Chapter - 8

The Social Outlook

Thus, some months passed. Arran and Abby were housemates because time had forced them to become so. Either they liked or disliked. People of the city discussed the issue frequently. Finally, the problem was also reported in some daily newspapers after some days or some months. Users who came for treatment at Jan Service Hospital also talked about it. It would often flash their face on a screen and oblige them to talk. They, also, wanted to know them very much and thus happily read any news about them.

The other day the editor of *The Social Outlook,* an influential monthly newspaper, came to see Abby and Arran. He interviewed them secretly and separately. Specifically, he interviewed Arran, which was put into the magazine as follows:

"Would you like to tell us something about your domestic life?"

"Not anything, rather many things."

"I want to know only about your married life."

"Yes! You can ask. No problem."

"What is life?"

"Life is a big book which is full of experiences sweet and bitter worth and evils joys and sorrows..."

"However, when I interviewed you immediately after your

marriage you had told me that 'life is a love and romance'. Now you seem changed. Can you say something about its reasons?"

"Life is a riddle. A very difficult riddle! They are unseen until one comes upon them – comes upon man. This is an unconscious reality and most of us do not grasp it. It's so strange and not known nor felt by anyone, including myself. Life is full of troubles. The sense of sexual love and romance is momentary."

"Can you say that the love marriage is successful?"

"This is a compromise between man and woman. This is a common matter. Everybody goes through the institution of marriage, a social one. That is how we carry out the biological role of humankind to perpetuate the Creation."

"I am not talking about sexual practice, but rather about the love marriage."

"Notwithstanding, the love marriage is not a transgression against nature, but the consequence of early excitement to sexual intercourse in the name of love. This is a question of general debate whether love marriage is a crime against the social contract formed by marriage or not. If practiced suitably with the supervision of the parents/guardian in terms of reality, there is nothing wrong with it."

"Why can you say 'premature passion'?"

"The love marriage lacks social support, and the journey of life is not possible without it because it passes through different stages through flowers and thorns."

"I want to know only the love marriage."

"It is a result of tenderness!"

"What is love?"

"Love is an ageless love that mankind binds to mankind and lays the foundation for a man's love for a woman and a woman's love for a man. Love is God."

"What do you mean by sex?"

"This is a method of generation for the prolongation of Creation. It is a biological act."

"Marriage?"

"Marriage is the holy of the holy of manmade institutions and no one is allowed to pollute this sacred institution. Now I know. Those who refrain from accepting its data will depart from peace so far as the rest of their lives. This is a worldly fact. A Thousand per cent true."

Following the interview, the editor further privately interviewed Abby as well.

"Does society affect human happiness?"

"Definitely! Society has a significant social influence on the happiness of man, as man cannot exist without it. Man is a social being. He cannot live alone."

"Does society also play any role in marriage? Is any value of it?"

"Surely! It plays an important role in marriage. In it, two human beings of different sexes join to live in peace and rest fulfilling their physical needs and strengthening social and moral values, and it is only possible if it gets social support."

"Which type of marriage do you like?"

"Arranged marriage...also love marriage, but after serious consideration avoiding tenderness and consent of parents or guardians, who had better experiences than the two persons of the tender age."

"Everywhere?"

"Yes."

"In which condition?"

"Everywhere. However particularly in Indian society where 99 percent of the population has one marriage experience. They live their life happily till the end of their life. This particular characteristic is present only in Indian culture and can be explained only by arranged marriages and very detailed scrutiny of every piece of information before the wedding vows – to be away from any post-marital problems."

"Do you like it?"

"Yes!"

"Yet you agreed to the wedding vow of the cohabitation marriage?"

"Blunder."

"Blunder?"

"Yes…blunder!"

"You expressed your ideas in favour of the love marriage previously, and you said that man and woman should have the right to decide their future independently. Now your view is quite different. Changed."

"Really! The arranged marriage!"

"Are you sure?"

"Surely my experiences reveal it."

"How?"

"In the arranged marriage, family, and the parents are better able to judge than the two men at a young age."

"Do you want to claim that a matrimonial household by arranged marriage really can bring the greatest happiness to the lifetime of man?"

"Yes! It is highly efficient to bring joy for life as long as possible in the world. It is not just, but also better than a love marriage."

"And the love marriage?"

"The love marriage is not worse. It is not fully a failure everywhere. The only downside to it is its lack of social support and no opportunity to take advantage of the experiences of family and friends. But, it is not to say that love marriage is redundant. Inter subjectivity between couples in love marriage does not replace couples in arranged marriage inter subjectivity. Never! I have its experiences. The institution of marriage has been built with most of the classical values of human life, for example, this is a sustainable system, although the partnership based on love marriage is an emotional binding, far from the reality of life.

"Is any idea about life?"

"Life is a machine which consumes sorrows."

"The world?"

"The world is covered in pied beauty...familiar and strange... roses and prickles."

Both interviews were reprinted in *The Social Outlook*, and then read by and debated across the Global North, South, and East. For and against the love marriage for and against the arranged marriage. The international media equally debated the topic on a wider scale and also organized a special programme under the 'Open the Mouth; Real India Speaks'. Men and boys in the urban areas wanted just for love marriage, old men and the literati were determined to choose it for the deadly Westernized culture, and so were they for Indianized culture.

On the other hand, Arran and Abby were living their life together. It was reported by a few that they were just passing time and she was conceived during that time. However, she kept this information to herself for three months. She kept its secret inside of herself, and she was not known to be pregnant. But it was impossible in the fourth month, and Dali guessed it. So, she asked her and she disclosed it.

Knowing it, Dali became serious about her safe pregnancy. After that, there was a decrease in strife in the family. She became happy and continued to wait for the day, on which there would be a baby in her lap who would cry in her lap saying 'Grandma. . . grandma..."

During the period of her pregnancy, Dali was happier than her. Abby was also happy, but not like Dali. Dali disclosed the secret of her happiness before Bali. Knowing it, he also became happy.

Dali began to guide her. Delicious food was given to her according to the food chart for a pregnant woman. This food chart was given to her by Dali. The food chart was pasted on the wall in her bedroom. Abby did this with such a happy disposition and Dali was "trying to make her feel good." Her mother-in-law did not let her do anything as per her will. She was registered in the maternity centre of the city, and she was under the guidance of her in-laws. The members of the medical staff also continued to visit to guide her, and she was enrolled on their register.

One thing was very important to say that all members of the medical staff and medical science were superseded by the experiences of Dali, and she guided her to do something or not to do anything. Meanwhile, it seemed that they had forgotten the past. Abby was on bed rest. In such a situation, Dali continued to go to the market and brought something special for her according to her likes and dislikes...according to her necessity. She accepted whatever was thrown at her, and sometimes Dali served her, too. Regional magic was also practised in Dali, which was common in the city for pregnant women.

Thus, six months elapsed in this way and they were expecting the arrival of a new member of the family. For that time, Dali was more to them than their servants and all was well. They were very happy. Strife was seldom observed but no one could deny that it was not only invisible but also imperceptible to anyone quite. Seven months of her pregnancy passed, and they were waiting for the rest two months. She maintained normal contact with the maternity centre and, according to her maternity card, was healthy and no defect was apparent. The doctors checked her regularly.

The report of her ultrasound showed as mentioned below:

"Everything is going well. No deficiency is seen. No abnormality is diagnosed. A foetus is normal in shape and size. Both kidneys are normal in shape and size. The pancreas is normal. The gall bladder is normal. The liver is normal in shape and size...."

Both the doctor and all the family members were happy with the presentation and they were ready for an auspicious day on the 9th month's date.

The day of waiting! How long it is! One can imagine it easily.

Unfortunately, a minor event brought the family to the lap of strife. It was Saturday. They were joyous and expecting the auspicious day after nine months. Abby had taken fast and she required apples. So, she asked Dali to fetch apples from the market. Arran had already left for the market, so she rang him to get it done and confirmed to bring it. But misfortune was not ready to take a break. It happened that he could not come back to his home in time due to some unavoidable reasons, and he brought it late at night. He presented it to her, but she threw it. She reported the refrained consumption of the apples in the evening. She was mad and her husband's family was not paying her any attention. However, Arran told her for the right reason that he couldn't get it in time. He was contrite about it and asked that she have the apples to eat, but she did not. Dali also tried to pacify her but in vain. Abby was not ready to listen to them. Nevertheless, she did not become upset and expressed herself in a calm and friendly manner.

She was too angry and said that she was not a witch to eat anything at any time. She had said to bring the apples during the day, but knowing, he did not do so. Thus, she said that he did not love her father, and hated her. According to her, he was her enemy and he wanted to kill her. She said to die herself, but she would not eat it. She loudly said that she would consume poison. She said to touch a live electric wire - also to jump into the road. She blamed that all of them did not like to let him live and all of them were the same. So, she had no will to live. She also said that Arran did not care for her. In addition, she explained that she was not his beloved; his beloved was the nurses. She was a widow and he provided for her at every visit and continued to go there. She was not only his nurse but also his mate. She said that she seemed well and Abby seemed old. Sometimes, Arran expressed this type of idea to her. Then she was lazy, black, fat, and bulky for him. He continued to use 'darling' before the wedding but changed it to "Abby". What was all this? Was this regard or humiliation? She said that she understood all this. She knew the matter of his mind and heart. Everything was known by her. She asserted that she was a tracker and everything could be tracked. She used to say it, everyone. Previously he used to say to her to bring stars from the sky for her before marriage, but then he could not bring even some apples in time. Abby told him in that situation, he was not to trust him, he was a cheat. She cradled him as the lowest in the world and the lowest person she had ever encountered in her entire life.

These ideas of Abby showed that now there was no place for Arran in her mind and heart. She was remembering her past and not understanding the meaning of practical life and the harsh realities of the world.

In the meantime, Arran was sitting having kept his hands on his head and he had no words to express. He was feeling guilty. He tried to pacify her in different ways to the best of his knowledge and said that he couldn't bring apples in time because he was treating some patients in an emergency condition. He guaranteed to avoid such type of errors in the future. However, she did not regard him as anything and shut the door. She also began to sob and weep. Dali also aimed at mellowing herself outwardly through the window of the windowed room, etc.

Dali also prayed aloud, "O my beloved daughter! Please pardon my son...please pardon all of us. O my House Goddess! Please listen to my prayer. Please excuse me. There will be no repeats of this type of error. O, Goddess! Please show mercy to us. We beg your pardon. This is just a trivial thing."

Nevertheless, she listened to them not a single word. Meanwhile, something novel was first encountered in the household. Anyone in the family was not using abusive words. Dali had kept her patience and was not agitated. She was taking the event as a process of normal life and family life. She was taking it as a common happening. Arran was also stoic and took the issue very, very seriously. He was outside the room, and outwardly sedating her. He was completely ordinary and heard her as an audience and asked her to knock on the door. But she did not do so. Despite all this, all of them were taking the issue easily and none was agitated or violent.

She persisted. Two days passed, but she ate nothing. On the third day, a new problem came to her she began to weep and cry because of pain in her abdomen area because of labour pain. See, the door was already broken and she ended up going to the hospital. She was admitted to an emergency ward. Doctors tried to treat her, but misfortune followed, and her pregnancy ended in miscarriage. Her parents also reached there and they consoled her. They were serious, but not upset, and explained it was a consequence of their destiny. They also suggested she forget the tragedy.

Although that was an unwelcome tragedy, the family was in control and they were handling it very serenely and patiently. The Arran and Abby's parents consoled them and recommended they live happily.

They said that it happened and it meant nothing in the general drama of life, and God would solve their problem. He watched over everything and solved all of their problems. He was their determiner. They also reported that they had also gone through that stage, and God will surely give them one problem sometime soon. They stated that their destiny was in the grasp of God and that He would hear them definitely and would favourably bless them.

There was a wide impact of all this on both of them, and they were living happily. They had forgotten their past. They were living in the moment and their future was buried there. However, others reportedly felt that their future could be found in the past. No matter what may be said or consoled, the history of the past is palpable in their features and their family.

Chapter - 9

God's Modern Story

Time continued to pass. They were residing in the family unit and no big problems except some petty problems were facing them. Dali suggested they hold a religious programme for listening to the story of God...either modern or ancient. She explained that if they give ear to the story of God, then God could redeem them from all griefs and pains in life. They, therefore, accepted her suggestion and held it.

It was Sunday - the eleventh day of the bright side of Vaishakh. At about 10 a.m. The priest came to their home to hold and narrate the modern *Harikatha*...the modern story of the Almighty. It started with the beep of a virtual alarm, not the carapace of the holy person. Instead of a holy man, the priest sat on a sandalwood sofa. All necessary items for the fulfilment of rituals were kept aside and Arran and Abby were sitting together on another big sofa which was also made of sandalwood. She had made her up in a famous beauty parlour in the city. He was in a blue jeans pantaloon and a red shirt, and she was in a blue jeans pantaloon and a yellow shirt, as for the daily practice of modern *Harikatha* it is common. Their undergarments were flower-cut and printed with various flower patterns. They wore handkerchiefs around their heads and the garment of Arran was tied fast with Abby's garment. They were sitting passively and doing what the priest was asking. Vatsyayana's *Kamasutra* lay not beside but on a holy table in advance of the *Gita.*

Some neighbours had been also invited to participate in it and they along with their family members were also sitting behind them and listening to the modern *Harikatha.* It was narrated part by part and the alarm was voiced by him according to its part. For one part it was voiced one time...and for the second part, it was voiced two times, and so on.

The priest was telling the narrative of God like this:

This is the story of a long time ago. There was a village in the most out of the way of the Kashmir valley, nestled in the peaks of the Himalayas. Its name was Joypore. There was a handsome man from a rich family. His name was Joy. He was very smart. His stature was seven feet and looked like a manifestation of the Almighty.

Joy was one of the dear sons of his parents and he studied in different ancient education centres of the highest level. He was loved by his mother. When he visited a former model school, the welcome was friendly. His shoes were decorated with diamonds and gold. His comb and pen were also made of gold. The buttons of his school uniform were made of diamond. He was enrolled at school in a gold-reinforced palanquin borne by bearers on their shoulders. A team of security staff followed his palanquin in the way. Other students of the school called him a "prince". As a prince! A unique type of school wallet full of romantic books was also decorated with gold thread. His smile was immortal.

Beauty was no less than Joy. She was a very smart girl, and she lived in Beautycounty, a village at the foot of Heaven Mountain. She was born into a very rich family and was very polite. People regarded her as 'Humbly'. She was a fairy child and seemed as beautiful as Helen. She kept using all the cosmetics that she could get at that young age. Whenever she went to a girls' school, it was deeply experienced by all the students. It seemed that the west wind had entered the school. Other students addressed her as a 'school star'. Her sandals were hill-added, and she was the only student in the school who used to wear such type of sandals because others were not allowed to do so and they, therefore, used to wear the wood-made sandals. Her school uniform was comprised of silk and was mounted with pearls gems, and metals. Thus, she glittered like gems and pearls even in the darkness.

When Joy grew young, he married Beauty. Lakhs of people participated in their marriage. What was not? Everything! After witnessing, the management, some people have questioned. Horses from Kabul...white elephants from Thailand...garments from Dhakka...perfumes from Arab...date-palm from gulfs...apples from Shalimar in Kashmir ...grapes from Sudan...

As soon as they got married, they moved out of their house to have their honeymoon trip in the hill city of Himachal Pradesh and reached Shimla. Following this city, they felt like they wanted to go to some beautiful places or natural attractions for aesthetic pleasure. So they went to Romantic Park, Chandigarh, the Khajuraho Temple, and other romantic spots. When they were returning from Khajuraho, they purchased Vatsayayan's *'Kamasutra'*. They also went to Sex Yoga and Sex Centre at the end of their trip.

When they were coming back from Khajuraho, they were very happy, and it seemed that they had attained the treasury of joy. They believed that it was only a trip to their life that provided happiness for them. They considered the Temple of Khajuraho as the best religious centre in the world which was able to provide heavenly joy to provide divine bliss for the life of man. They stated that other religious buildings are allowed only to be perceived without being looked at or touched directly, and worshipped idols in the *Temple of Khajuraho* were a direct expression of divine or goddess amoral teaching, as well as an accurate portrayal of the life of humankind.

Several years later they still lived in Joypore. Time changed as happened to each person. Their attraction to one another decreased. As with this illusionary condition, an array of ideas started flooding their thinking in such a way. But in the meantime, Beauty became pregnant. So, her in-laws cared for her as was possible for them. Unfortunately, after some months, she was aborted. Its main cause was family strife. They, therefore, fell into the ocean of sorrows and there was no good relation between Joy and Beauty between wife and husband. Conflicts were frequent, and they could not stop it. They lost peace and the rest of their life. It appeared that the peace and rest would not befall them but only at a time from their demise.

However, all this, they were living their days and hours. They were regularly consoled by their elders. Their attraction to one another continued to decrease, and they were too unhappy with their life. In being in times of distress and suffering they were trying to find what brought joy to their lives, but not a single light of joy was found.

They had also discontinued fulfilling their duties because both Joy and Beauty worked as the 'Chief Minister' and the 'Deputy Minister' respectively. Joy was one of the fine and lovable heads in the court of the Kashmiri king. Since of his integrity, and plainness (present in the age), the king was fond of him. He received several awards in court for his courting and insincere praise. The king loved him enough and also sought his advice even on his private matters. He was a public phenomenon, and in the time of Joy's service in the court of the king, the income available to the King increased by 75 per cent. Joy was seen as a messiah of the tenants of the kingdom. The king felt proud of him and if any problem caused him, he was over sure that Joy would solve the problem. His family was considered the most civilized family in the kingdom, and there was a family-type relationship between Joy and the king of Kashmir. Only because of his true service to the king, Beauty was also appointed as the 'Minister'. Over time, she also became obedient to the king and gained enough popularity. Her actual service was known to be well-regarded, and the king often consulted with her in matters of high importance. During their service period, they made enough money.

Despite all this, they were not happy with themselves. The tussle frequently occurred, and no solution came to them.

One day, they were sitting on a sofa and kept their hands, they were falling into a dilemma and were thinking about their future. In the meantime, an old man with having long white beard and hair came to them and wanted to know the cause of their despair.

The stranger asked them, "Tell me! How! Why! What! From where! Tell me! Recognize me! Know me! Know about my right and might...my rule and regime. What I am! I think, now you recognize me."

They recognized him. They understood that He was God.

They said, "O my Lord! O, my God! We know you! We recognise you well! You are the Supreme Power! The Supreme! You know everything – everything about us. We need not say anything. We are helpless and we have no words. But if you will allow me to say, I shall make it all known."

God said, "Yes...Tell me."

Listening and seeing Him, they became very happy. They wanted to gain His boon. They said:

"O, my God! We have lost the joy of our life. We have tears and tears. There are only tears for us. Joy is far away from us. It does not seem anywhere. We are suffering now. We were happy in the past. But we are bleeding presently. We have no children. Who will survive us? Who will possess our property after our death? We are compelled to suffer – compelled to die. We are tied to death in a living state. We have discontinued fulfilling our duty. We are not happy with anything we receive from the king's court as we cannot meet our demands solely on wages. Salary is nothing for us. The amount of bribes is not enough presently. Its trend is going below. Now, a few people offer a bribe to us. The amount of the bribe was five thousand per cent times more than the salary previously. Others play with lakhs and we play with thousands. What is the value of thousands in this age? You know it well. At the moment we are sitting on those chairs which are labelled as negative chairs in the bribery field. We can no longer create phantom bills of a thousand times the real one. The monarch's treasury is managed by a different minister, who is always, always honest, and in this situation, we, whether it be for lack of another piece of the king's pie or just to be able to accept some of the petty bribes, whether from the Buddhist king or others less readily corruptible, can, at least, face the consequences, and at the same time profit from them a little. We have palatial buildings in only two cities, while others have a dozen palatial buildings in metropolitan cities of India. We have only lakhs, others only crores all because their chairs are 'bribe plus', not crores. Our chairs are 'bribe minus and minus'. We, therefore, pray you to award us 'bribe plus plus' chairs, palatial buildings in metropolitan cities, a dozen children, quintals of gold and diamond, divine bliss, a golden chance to enjoy with fairies on the earth and heaven…and all other which is possible to be awarded by you."

God listened to their woes and sorrows. He said:

"All is right. I grant everything to you. Everything! But you will have to do only one thing...you will have to listen to modern *Harikatha.* As you perform it, everything will be granted automatically...everything will be at your hand. You have also to do one another thing, you have to donate fifty per cent of the amount of the bribe to the priests. Fifty-fifty is a good standard for disclosing the amount of bribe, which is widespread all over the world. The effect will be that there will be total growth in your family."

God continued to say:

"They, therefore, did so and the result was that they entered the empire of divine bliss, and they possessed 'bribe plus and chairs', palatial buildings, crores of rupees, fairies in your lap to enjoy sexual pleasure, etc. In this way, they began to live happily, and then they were followed by divine bliss. Woes and sorrows were unfathomable miles away from them."

Abby and Arran breathed a sigh of relief after listening to the contemporary *Harikatha.* They were tremendously happy and wanted eternal happiness in the future. They expected that the rest part of their life would be full of bliss. Their sense of happiness, peace, and rest was felt in every walk of their life. There was no tussle or strife. They performed their daily work, and the wound of the conflict looked healed completely.

The contemporary *Harikatha* has brought peace and tranquillity not only to Arran and Abby but also to their parents. Their family atmosphere is very tranquil and comfortable.

Chapter - 10

The Child of Strife

There was a sense of peace and quiescence all around the family. The sense of joy was easily felt. It appeared that there was a "condition to effect a complete transformation" in Arran's and Abby's lives. In that state of quietude, she became pregnant for a second time.

Thus, they began to wait for the auspicious day. Her mother-in-law continued to guide her. On a few occasions, she used to fetch her to the hospital to get the consultation of a gynaecologist for her safe delivery. She further made Abby comply with everything that the doctor instructed her, and she was not permitted to act according to her desires. The gynaecologist advised her to take a tablet of folic acid and iron daily. She was also recommended to eat palatable food, deionised water for her depolluted body, tetanus vaccine, greens and vegetables, head side lower bed, full bed rest and so on. She did, and Dali taught her along each step. In this way, six months of her pregnancy passed. The seventh month was on the way to it. They were in suspense for the first week, following the ninth month. Everything was going well and understood. Some aspects of modern *Harikatha* also entered their life.

A well-known astrologer of Varanasi had prepared Abby's horoscope and whatever was said by him to her parents for fulfilling the rituals after the birth of Abby, had been fulfilled under the guidance of eleven Brahmins of the same place.

However, one unexpected event that was not recorded in her horoscope occurred. It was dawn the dawn of Saturday the combination of the Mars and the Moon planets according to Abby's horoscope.

During the same morning/time, her husband went outside and started a morning walk and she stayed at home in the bedroom. Her in-laws were in other rooms in the same dwelling. Meanwhile, she was talking over her mobile phone very slowly, and he listened to her as follows:

"I am living here half-heartedly. The body is still here, the soul is to you and for you as also was "sold" before my union. You are my 'dream boy'. He is nothing to me. He can be considered by me a bedfellow. I loved you...and still I love you... and will continue to love you. No one can stop me from doing so. Be sure. Believe me. I will continue to meet you secretly. No one will know. He is for name, and you are for work and fame. I still worship your photograph daily at my home very secretly and no one knows all this. I am a kibitzer, and I fight my in-laws merely to break out of this cage and be a part of your life. The time for us comes when we will join once again...we will meet once again. You are not my lover, but rather also my heartbeat... my God too. I look forward to having my youth with you next Valentine's Day. I am sure. I will enjoy your handsome body. Your lap is just like paradise. When I remember my past with you, my condition becomes critical. I usually dream...dream about you and our love affairs. Do you remember the first day when you had enjoyed in the inn, and you had turned my body fit and heat? Sometimes, I also mutter about you while sleeping. However, I am not as free as was the case in the past due to social ties but, I know that no one can tie is spirit, which only belongs to you. I love you. I'm making a tremendous effort to be unburdened of the spell of Arran and so expect to be free from him shortly. He is not in a position to make my body cool. Now Arran has gone out for a morning walk and none is listening to me..."

All this was heard by Arran secretly, and she could not know because when he knew that she was talking over the phone to someone, he concealed himself in the garden on her room side. He listened to her everything very quietly and discretely. Listening to her, however, he was wildly agitated, but trying hard to stay calm. When it became intolerable for him, he ran fast towards her bedroom, and he found that the room was closed inwardly. He, therefore, told her to open the door. He started to threaten and scold in a shrill voice. The door was opened, but before opening the door, she deleted the dialled number as Arran said.

Having entered the bedroom, he first snatched her mobile phone and tried to get the then dialled number and the name of the person to whom she was talking. But he could not get it. He, therefore, told her to disclose the dialled number and the name of the person, but she refused to do so and said that she was not talking to anyone rather she was dreaming about all that mentioned above. However, he could not (yet) accept her, and he started to assault her. There was a tussle. Hence, she also beat him. Her in-laws ran fast towards her to save him, and they interfered with him. In the meantime, she gave birth to a baby in the seventh month of her pregnancy. On the other hand, he kept on crying and wanted to kill both Abby and her foetus. He attempted to do the best of his ability. But a number of his neighbours along with her in-laws, who were assembled there, saved her and the infant. So, he failed to do so.

A heavy crowd assembled there. They began to discuss the issue in different ways. The other individuals were surprised by the critical state of a gentry family in the city. On the one side, there was strife, and on the other side, the birth of a baby by her. Later on, some people took them to the hospital. However, he did not reach them and continued to roar in front of them.

He said, “She is corrupt...she is not my wife...she is not my daughter...she is a prostitute. She was pregnant, but not with my child, but rather with her partner’s. I saw her red-handed having a secret chat with her paramour on her mobile phone. She was talking very romantically. She has cheated me...she has spoiled my life. When she wanted to keep up her tryst with him, why got married to me?

She has illicit relations with her cousin's husband. According to her telephonic dialogue, her body is here, but her spirit is with her lover. She was telling all this to her boyfriend on the phone. I listened to her directly. I continued to say in the past that she loved someone else and that she was corrupt, but no one was ready to believe me. She refused usually. But now it is quite clear. The fact is before us...before all of you. Society should come forward to support me...to help me. I noticed all this in the past, but she usually deleted the dialled or received objectionable contact numbers. All of us know that the fact is never hidden and comes out one day. Now it has come out. She kept some stuff hidden, and she continued to do this, although from today her secrets have been breached. Now I will not let her enter my house. I will not accept the child. She is not by me. A DNA test may be performed. Abby is an adult prostitute and her own child is the product of prostitution..."

He said all this very loudly to the crowd assembled there. On the one hand, he was thundering at his home and on the other hand, the police, the Children Welfare Commission, the Human Rights Commission, and the Women Commission took the issue seriously and the members of staff related to these organisations reached the hospital for enquiry. They considered it as the rarest among rare issues. Many people assembled there. They showed mercy and sympathy for Abby and her child.

Getting her pathetic situation, some people began to weep because there were some wound spots on her body. Some of them consoled Abby. A person in their midst is guaranteed to assist them in such a serious circumstance. Some people were too agitated against Arran, and they said to burn him if they found him. There was no one in favour of him. All were criticizing him in the same way.

The media persons also reached there and knew everything in detail. The news was presented in the form of headlines in an interesting manner. People discussed the news broadly, and several editorials were written and published on the issue. People easily pass their time by reading news related to the issue of Abby and Arran.

There was no one either man or woman, who was in favour of Arran. All criticized him. Every one of them abused him and told him that he had blotted out his father's image. They said that if he had no love for his child why he had given birth to her...if he had no respect for the woman why he had married Abby? Every passerby believed that he had made a mistake in winning against his wife in this kind of circumstance when she was carrying, and neither father should incur such a barbarous act, as he did to his wife. They did not want to be convinced that Abby was communicating with somebody over the telephone and they claimed she was dreaming that he had taken away the right on the very basis that every person had the right to dream and nobody has and cannot prevent anyone from dreaming.

The condition of Abby and her child was stable. Doctors were very cautious about their recovery and minute by minute they were monitoring them. According to them, they were out of danger, and they were recovering their health fast. The government had also directed the hospital administration to treat them in a very careful and serious way. So, the doctors on duty were very alert and monitored her situation very carefully. They prescribed recently discovered standard medicines used for easy recovery that were imported from overseas.

The police also went to the place and the hospital and registered a case against Arran and all of his family members at different sections of the Indian Penal Code and the Dowry Act. They questioned her extensively about the event and her statements were also entered into the police file, that is, audio recorded with sound on a camera. She was telling all of it in fashion, in addition to crying bitterly.

She said to the police that…at about 4 am, she was sleeping in her bedroom. It was too cold, and so she had covered her whole body with a quilt. In the meantime, her cruel husband went for a morning walk. So she shut the room to the outside world internally, and once more she slept as she invariably does. So, there was no more in her memory. In the meantime, she dreamt. Perhaps! Perhaps her cruel husband listened to her dream. He came back and found the door opened by me. She saw him and started to be abused and beaten the moment she opened the door. He beat her badly. He awarded shoes, sandals, and rods to her body. He was assisted by her in-laws. They were supporting him. Only because of their cruel acts against her, she gave birth to a baby in the seventh month. Now they had crossed the border and she was quite unable to tolerate them. She said that she could not live with them, and she would find them cut into pieces by butchers. Abby told them all of this to the police, but in reality, it was quite different.

They repeated asking, however, if she did so over the phone with her beau in a shy, discreet way...or not.

She refused flatly and said that...no...no...She was in a dream and she was not in conversation with her boyfriend or anyone else on the phone. He had no lover, rather he had many beloveds. He had many wives or bedfellows in the hospital. They acted as a nurse, and in so doing also fulfilled his sexual needs. They were not members of his nursing staff only, but rather his bed partners also. He was to appear in society as a husband only, but the truth was, Abby was nothing. He had hundreds of wives. He also visited brothel(s) and had sexual relations with his elder brother's wife and her younger sister. He strolled by women's colleges in the city and romantic parks. She was not corrupt like him. He was over-corrupt. People knew him. The members of the medical staff of the hospital knew him and his deeds. Nothing was hidden. Consequently, she rationalized her poor work and concealed the same to hide the truth and her secret dalliance with her boyfriend.

The police also questioned her, the second time, when the policemen went to her home and found out that she was on the phone, being held by someone. He was, however, upset, and, therefore, started to beat and mistreat her.

Listening to them, she was in a tangle and started to accuse them. She blamed that they were partial and his supporters. She also said that they were misogynists so they were talking in his favour. She explained that they were backing him and because they were a woman, they were not backing Abby, but pushing Arran. It was no doubt the case that a woman against a woman is an adversary. She said not to argue, rather help her not him. According to her, male-kind was an enemy of womankind. They exploited women. They ruined women. All of this was shamelessly and crudely expressed to the police by Abby. However, the policemen wanted to handle the dilemma sincerely and objectively.

They said, “I will undoubtedly investigate the issue impartially, and we want to know the facts.”

Abby said to express something privately.

She said, “I will reveal it privately...”

Next to the SP, the Chairman of the Children Welfare Commission also arrived. She asked her about the issue in different ways in a private room. Meanwhile, Abby was groaning, as if suffering an unbearable amount of pain. She questioned her many times, and her answers were shown to her and were videographed, as per the desire of the Police Inspector. Following her inquiry into the problem she went on to the media and articulated her thoughts as follows:

The Chairperson said that...Not surprisingly, it was an absolute abuse of children’s rights, since their rights could take place in their wombs, too. They had the right to remain safe. Unfortunately, however, Arran, the father of the baby, did not raise her. As such, he was guilty of violating children’s rights. The exploitation of Abby was the exploitation of her baby in her womb. A mother had a fundamental right to protect her foetus even in her womb. But she had become unable to protect her foetus. They reported that they had witnessed the sadistic behaviour of her husband and of her relatives. As a result, she had delivered a baby by the beating. She might have died. As if the Almighty had spared her, now she was laughing in her mother’s lap. One could see with perfect clarity that she was somebody born into discord – not only a family conflict but she might have been born without the benefit of her mother’s womb pregnancy as well. So, the Chairperson said that she would go to the police to write against Arran and her in-laws for taking the stern action against them as possible under the prescribed rule of the Indian Penal Code and the Children Protection Act. Children were our future, and no one had the right to play with our future or to misbehave with any child. Therefore not only the Chair but the Chairpersons also found him guilty of the problem.

After her press release, she went to the police station and submitted her report to the police, and they told her to take stern action against them, while the police personnel was already very active. They guaranteed they would hit the guilty ones with the strictest sanctions.

The Women's Commission was working on it also as the most exceptional of the exceptional cases, it was treated as an issue in a battle against women's right to use. It, therefore, decided to get the guilty persons punished. Its response was more resistant and classified the problem as a serious crime against women. The reaction to it was tougher (that is, more difficult) than any other organization or individual.

As their Chairperson saw her plight, the blood of both burned hot and bubbled like an earthen pot. Her face became red and fiery. Small boils rose to her face. She seemed angrier than Abby. The self stated that her physical assault was unacceptable by anyone that she would be retaliating against Arran and her parents at an extreme level, and that no one would do such a crime against other women in the future.

She declared that…now women were not in such a situation to bear the atrocity of males. It was enough. However, it was still tolerable for women but became intolerable to them. Now they had no patience and no passion for males. They expressed that they should all burn them...they too had a right to enjoy themselves like men. If men were free then women had a right to be free. Men went anywhere, so women had also the right to go anywhere. No one could snatch their rights. If men talked to anyone, then women had also the right to talk to anyone in any condition or in any way. They could also participate in unsocial sexual activities. Therefore, she motivated women, saying that they could also do well at it seriously, without any fault in the matter. If it was necessary and both were agreeing, nothing was wrong in doing so. But if Abby had spoken by phone, none of the crimes would have been committed, as social rights facilitate communication with all. A woman had a right to have several men for sexual purposes. What was wrong with it? All human beings have the right to enjoy. Males also did all this. According to her, the fact was that Abby was not talking to anyone, rather she was dreaming only. Arran had misapprehended the true issue and maltreated her. He had a history of severe violence against her, so she had gone into labour in the seventh month of her pregnancy instead of the ninth month. She was quite gentle and honest. She was a lady of morality, and she was over chaste...a thousand per cent. She had made her share of her husband's wants, as anyone has the justification to do it, as anyone can make use of. She had put up with her husband's abuse and brutality. So, she was tolerant. But despite all this, Arran had attacked her. So, he was an enemy of womankind. She would not live with him. She possessed all constitutional rights and would go for justice in the court of law...she would stand for justice. All the women were with her. It was a case of almost a case of vanishing with the commission, never encountered by the commission to date. Thus, she would be given a separate case reported against Arran and the rest of her in-laws. She also reported that wounds to her own body should be visible and easy to see. All women had come to the edge of their patience. She would demand the severest punishment by the court for him and others, and she would take her to her office and register her complaints before a video camera. The pictures of her wound would be also sketched and presented to the woman judge in the court. At present, women are in no position to be treated as puppets for men, since they are men's equals. They were not inferior. Women were the same, but this idea did not mean that they would labour pulling rickshaws or become coolies. It is necessary to bring it into the minds of every woman in the world. Thus, she encouraged her to present several ideas.

The Human Rights Commission was also involved and it took the issue very seriously, its members went to the hospital and interviewed her in a room closed to the public before the presence of a video camera. In the meantime, she talked to them using her thoughts and she cried a lot. They consoled her and she could say something. But she began to weep again and again, and they consoled her again and again. Anyway, they were able to transcribe her confidences on a record over four hours and were released to the press.

The Chairperson of the commission said that...after serious and impartial investigation of the case, they had concluded that this was the meanest deed and quite intolerable for any civilized society. It was inhumane and Arran had sullied all of humanity. Abby had been beaten by him badly, so she had given birth to a baby in the seventh month...before the natural period of delivery. Now the whole of humanity was in deep danger. Humanity had been turned. Time was changed. But no one had the right to go against the law...to go against humanity. Arran had violated all the established systems of society. The commission noted that any such problem never appeared before it. This was a heinous crime against humanity. Each woman had the right to protect her foetus. However, Arran took away from Abby this natural and legal right. As a result, the US Human Rights Commission also held Arran responsible, but not Abby.

The following day, was the day of the daily newspapers, with the readers eagerly reading through various newspapers.

Abby's parents also arrived at the hospital with a stack of newspapers in their hands. They were becoming out of control and were using offensive language towards Arran and his parents. They disclosed that they had collected bags of rupees to burn both him and his parents, and would go to any lengths or means to fulfil any wish for their dearest daughter, Abby. The media men assembled there and posed different questions to them, and they replied boldly while she was weeping.

To the press, they claimed Abby was their heartbeat, and they would not allow it to be extinguished...they would not let her suffer or weep. She had come to this world not to suffer, but rather enjoy. If Arran had not brought both happiness and with it the problems of her life, this would not be a topic of much concern to them or her. There were many Arran-like persons. They were better than him. He was not only in this wide world. She had the right to do anything for the fulfilment of her joy. She had a fundamental right to talk to anyone over the phone or directly. She had the right to reject or to accept. It fell under the right to expression. So, who had the right to snatch her fundamental rights? If she was on the phone with anyone, what was the issue? It was under the right to expression. All had the freedom to speak his or her mind to whomever. So, there was nothing wrong with it. He continued to torture her. However, it was no longer bearable for them and Arran could not be allowed to conscript her human rights. Abby would not kneel before him. She was no more a doll or plaything than a partner she was, however. However 'is' had now become 'was' and she could never imaginatively recall how to go back to Arran. They would return her to their home and would chirp and she would stay with them.

Listening to them, she began to weep bitterly. But her parents consoled her, saying, "...do not weep...We're going to burn him and his parents in a kiln."

They assured her not to go to Arran and resolve her life's many issues. They reported that joy would return to her life again. Also, Abby was still not comfortable going back to her home. She said that they would kill her if she went there, and for his safety, there was only one to go to her mother's home.

She told her parents that she would also go to their home and would never go near Arran. She married him unknowingly. She failed to understand him. It was a blunder. She would pass the best part of her life with them, as God had given everything to them and not to Arran. She promised that she would die at their feet. This was her final decision.

Saying all this, she became unconscious, and it seemed that she was dead. Her parents started to get too depressed and cried because she was confirmed to be dead. They then told the doctors, who immediately visited her. They injected her and in a matter of moments she regained consciousness. Getting all this, her parents consoled her once again.

They said not to weep... move towards them...and they would be happy getting her back. They said all this, addressing her as their 'darling'. They were so fortunate that they had such a moralistic child, Abby, and such a fine and moralistic child could hardly be born. They promise her that they will not forgive them. They were sure! They also promised that they would burn Arran alive. They said that Abby was a gentlewoman and only because of this virtue, she was compelled to suffer. She had no evil. They suggested she keep patience. Everything would be in her favour. Policemen were very busy and had reached the formality of ageing. They had already been brought a large and heavy envelope. It was enough for them. A quite overwhelming account of the case had been recorded not only against Arran but also in the case of her other in-laws. Now, where would he go? Where will he live? They would heavily beat him with shoes, and even in the police basement. He'd be kicked about at a junction. The policemen were in their search, and they would send them to jail. However, before this, they would have them burn in hell, and they would be denied entry to this world. They were loaded with cash, and so could purchase the court of law. They declared that they had stacks of money and could buy many of their sons-in-law a lot better than Arran and men such as him did the cleaning of their shoes and sandals respectively. Arran did not know them. They could purchase judges and their justice. Justice was bought in India. They knew all this. Therefore, they are happy with their daughter and instead of putting their daughter on the track towards morality, they are so obviously happy to throw her on the wrong way where there were on and thorny ways.

Chapter - 11

Let Me Love

Some months passed. Thunder and lightning also ended. The amount of anger decreased below and the body became cold. Newspapers were read and thrown. Editorials were written, read, viewed, reviewed, and forgotten. People forgot it and started to fulfil their daily routines. Their discussion ended. Abby and her child both recovered and were discharged from the hospital. Abby moved in with her parents and started to live with them. She was quite sure that her parents would bring her happiness, and her brain and soul were inflated with hopes and expectations. She was very pleased with them and spent her leisure time with her child and her relatives.

In this way, three months passed. She began to repeat history. She began to go to nightclubs and lived there till late at night. Her parents supported her and told her to go there to be refreshed to recover her health. And her rosy smile was naturally apparent. Her mother, Lara became happy seeing her pleasing mood and patted her for her move.

Lara addressed her saying 'o my darling daughter' and said that then she seemed like a girl of fourteen. Fully of fourteen! She said how beautiful her darling daughter was! For her, she was like a fairy. She said to go to the nightclubs daily to be refreshed because she remained in tension at home. The new look would help her to remarry. Outwardly, the breeze was giving her a lift because she got too idle at home. Grief is the legacy of God's penalty, and sorrow only had to be endured with a merry heart. Later on, there may be new things, since time has passed. She explained that men are the puppets of time. She proposed a good timeframe and then they would discuss her future.

During the second (rehabilitation) phase stage of her journey to return to health she would frequently go to beauty shops. Specifically, she did not go to ordinary beauty shops; instead, she went to "Ever Beauty", a famous lady beauty shop in the city. Its result was that she seemed very nice. Her mother regarded her as a 'fairy child'. No one believed that she was the mother of one child, and she was forty-three years old. She bought several foreign cosmetic items from different companies through online shopping. They were very costly. Some of her boyfriends and girlfriends visited her home; and according to her, they were her well-wishers. A group of young men would go to the mother's house just once to see her. Some persons also moved around her clubs. Others saw her as a "Magnetic Girl" because of her charismatic style and her beauty.

Because of this, boys were easily attracted to her, and she got several messages daily, and she used to read and enjoy. However, one message was enough liked by her, and it was saved on her mobile phone. This was a message sent by a club member and addressed her as a "Magnetic Girl", and himself as a "Bee Boy." She always listened to this message, because she used to carry it with her mobile telephone next to her chest. When she read it, she lost in thinking. At that moment, it was as if she had forgotten her history of fighting.

This way, days went by and she kept on making up her look. Those days, no move was seen to rejoin Arran.

On the other hand, a bail application for Arran and his kin was approved, enabling them to live their own lives on their terms. He also could not approach her, and he decided to remarry. For example, he told some of his members in the club that he wanted to get married. They supported his decision and said that he was right having taken his wife out of his life. They said that he should marry any woman as soon as possible without delay. He also advertised his bio-data in 'Matrimonial Columns' as follows:

A bridegroom wants to remarry:

Name: Arran

Age: 44

Caste: No bar

Profession: Service (Doctor)

Qualification: MBBS, MD

Income: 2 lac rupees per month

Contact No: 1000022000 (Round the clock)

Personality: Handsome

This advertisement was published in a very famous newspaper. Having looked into the matrimonial columns, several individuals reached out to him, and several proposals of varying degrees were delivered to him. Some were very important. Some belonged to their teens. Seeing such proposals, he became very happy. His mood changed – despair into hope. He started imagining himself as a young teen, so had he been asked sometimes for suggestions. He thought that he wasn't wrong to have written about his marriage as published prior. He believed that such a golden opportunity shall not slip through his fingers. He both observed proposals and also interviewed several of them. Their photographs were also looked into by him in different ways. Several questions were posed to them. From the one hundred and seventy proposals, seven were chosen. He observed them and seven days passed.

Finally, he decided to marry Dolly. Both Arran and Dolly knew one another too. Dolly became very happy to pass that tough examination held by Arran. She felt like a very lucky girl and when he agreed with her firstly to marry, she revealed her ideas to her friends in the club very happily.

She said, "I am lucky number '1'. I am very fortunate. Aha!"

Other members of the club also supported her. Her happiness was uncontrollable and one could easily feel it by seeing her look. Wherever she turned she used to share all of that with her friends. Her language became very rhetorical. She was a scientist, but she spoke in the form of the *belles lettres* (i.e. some time afterwards, Dolly and Arran both found the courage to tell their parents their thoughts. That very day, Arran was very happy. He seemed fully changed. It seemed that nothing wrong had happened to him. Such pleasure was felt by him after months. Looking at his happy demeanour, his parents inquired about his happiness. So, he could not control his passion. Words spontaneously began to come out from his tongues.

He replied addressing 'o my dad! O, my mama!' A piece of very good news for his parents! He explained that he would allow Abby to go free from their house. Forget her quite! Forget the black bitch. She had burnt them – she had spoiled them. If she came again, she would kill them. He also reported that they were bleeding, and they were evident in all areas of their house. Now he had a suitable match...a girl, who was in her fourteen. She was ready to marry him. He also said that that match would erase their pains and tears. He also said that he had selected a girl of fourteen whose name was Dolly, who was the result of the hard attempt of his hard work as a pathfinder. She would turn their house into a paradise, and divine bliss would enter their home. He thought that when she came, their property would improve because she was a girl, voracious in her genius, and was able to give a talk on any subject with ease. He was full of praise for her, and he commented that she was an outstanding science student and it was impossible to stay ahead of her. He held as pure as Savitri. It seems that she was a goddess. Her father was a millionaire. There were many young men in the rows to gain her, but they failed, and he could gain her heart after a hard toil. He felt like a lucky number one, so he had won her, otherwise, she would have enlightened another man he was fortunate...they were fortunate, so they had got such a golden chance. So, he suggested they register her in their family. If a good result occurs, then Abby should attempt suicide. He had the presumption that if she learned of his remarriage he would consume poison, as he had witnessed the usual cases. He thought that she would live in hell, and they would live in a house like heaven.

Bali listened to him with very attention and pondered the problem for a few minutes. In the meanwhile, he was very serious.

He considered what would have to be done in order to be in such a state. He only cared about an option for family peace and tranquillity. He had nothing else to do when his daughter-in-law filed a case against them all.

On the other side, however, his son had not been legally separated from Abby. However, she lived with her parents and was not ready to live with her husband or to compromise on the case filed by her. All this was hunting his mind. He had passed more than half of his age. In other words, he decided to move on after careful thought and after reflections of his own experiences. He was highly distressed and no longer wished to deal with any further issues.

He said later on, "We must forget her. Her place should not be taken by anyone. That may be Dolly or someone else. For how much time will we wait? Will we die without any daughter-in-law in our family? Who will survive us? Who will look after us? Who will possess our property? But there is a serious problem. It is also impossible legally since you only got divorced now. But Abby is dead, and she has to be divorced, otherwise, according to the Hindu Marriage Act, your marriage will be illegal. There is one other issue, Dolly is only 14 years old and it is illegal to marry someone under eighteen years. She is underage."

But Arran said very boldly that he was ready to face any situation. He was sure and boasted, that nobody would hurt him. He explained that the statutes were kept in libraries, and they were not observed in everyday life. He was sure that there would be no problem caused by anyone as he was a well-known person in the city and many persons were working in courts and police departments who were once cured by him in his hospital in a serious condition. They had told him to give any chance for their service if he required it. However, he has not taken advantage since then.

However, Arran held a firm belief that Abby could not hurt them. He said that no one would harm them because they were not playthings. They were not rustics, and all knew them. No one had such ability. They knew a solution that they would not disclose socially and legally. This was a matter of their understanding. They would never accept it in court. This was the only option, or he would grow old, and he would continue to move around the courts for her divorce. That century would elapse, in that process, without their daughters-in-law. It was not simple to kiss the feet of Abby. He said that who would lick her feet to soften her? Now she was living in the world of dreams in the sky, which would be never true and she would die. So, they thought they should not wait for her - for such a witch who had spoiled their life.

However, Bali was not quickly prepared to embrace his feet to depart for his marriage without careful thought. So, he was fallen into a dilemma and was very anxious. No voice was coming from his mouth. But he viewed the issue in a moderate way which could be proper for him and the family. He was not sure of his decision. There was no certainty, and he was in a state of dilemma. He considered his age and stage and the possibility of coming up with a solution. He recalled his former state of pleasure and present state of distress and pain. He concluded the matter in that state of despair and frustration.

When he spoke to Arran very quietly that he was old, he wasn't in a position to wait for her and he wasn't able to put up with her. He had no desire to face further complications of litigation. He had made enough money. Everywhere no way had not been trialled by her to get a result. In any way...anyhow...either right or wrong. He did not think about it. However, at this time, there was no place for Bali's money. However, this did not imply that he was against Arran's decision but rather that he was in favour of it and Bali wanted to see him always well, that is, happy. His permission was for himself, but he had to make his own decision to get married again or not. He had already decided to marry Abby and they had never advocated for love marriages, but he wouldn't heed me. Its result was that their breath had been stopped. In the past, he thought to make money anyway and did so, but it went in vain. There was no one to survive him. Now he wanted to live in peace and rest, and he did not require money. He just wanted to die in quiet and sleep...not to live for money-funny.

However, Arran was hopeful about their bright prospects together with Dolly and wished to marry Dolly as soon as possible. He was delighted by Dolly, and they were looking forward to sharing a home and enjoying love, peace, and sleep. He wanted to enjoy the next wedding night with Dolly. He never wanted to let the golden chance go out of his hands. He also made fancies that he would enjoy the bodily charm of a woman, who was very beautiful and also in her teenage. He felt in the right that he was lucky, and so the opportunity had occurred to him.

So, Arran said to his father not to worry and that would fulfil his all desires. His father's money either right or wrong, would not go in vain. He was sure, he would be survived. He could face every complication. No one would harm them. Were they grasses, which would be grazed by Abby? He would teach her a lesson about her pride. He suggested to his father not to worry. He would not die alone he would not die issueless and would fulfil all of Bali's desires. He was quite sure.

On the one hand, Arran was using fast the threads for his remarriage and on the other hand, Dolly was weaving the threads of her marriage to him. She expected to live in peace and rest with him after her marriage. The movement of her feet was superfast as people said and such a movement was never seen previously. She felt proud that she would marry one of the rich men in the city. She seemed confused and often dreamt in the night when asleep.

One night, she was sleeping with her mother. Meanwhile, she dreamt as mentioned below:

"How pleasant your lap is! Aha! Arran! Aha! You are in my heart. Aha! What is the day with you? I am better than Abby. You are not only my lover, but also my heartbeat. You are in my inner chamber of the heart. How deep your love is! Your love is immortal! How immortal your lap is! Your kiss is also immortal. I will not let you go anywhere. Let me sit in your lap. Let me kiss. Let me, love. Aha! How sweet! How blissful! Aha! Arran!"

All this was heard by her mother. Listening to her, she was astonished and fell into thinking. The whole night passed, but she could not sleep and continued to think about her dreams. The next morning she was sober, and when Dolly rose, she beckoned her over and sat her on her lap. Dolly came to her and sat in her lap. Her mother asked her about her dreams. To begin with, she did not make a single statement and refused, she denied any knowledge about her dream. But her mother continued to tell her to disclose the secret of love, and anyhow she became ready to disclose.

She reported, "O mama, is the hour that our happiness has gotten into our hand. Now we have got a platinum chance. There is a platinum package for us. But if we lose it we'll never get it back."

She told her mother very happily that if she would allow it, Dolly was prepared to make a statement about her selection of his partner. He was a prince and seemed like a god. He was a man of sincerity and honesty and was overwhelmed by virtues, and a person like him was rarely seen. Fortunately, she had won his heart, and having seen her, he used to become very passionate and saw her from bottom to top. He was ready to marry her then and there. He desired to get a divorce from his wife, who filled his life with pain and despair. He had already been permitted by his parents to do so, and they were waiting for the permission of Dolly's parents. When let them pertain, they would get the wedding cravat and those would, using the same long-awaited world of bliss, enter that world. Dolly thought they would permit her to permit them to do so. Her mother knew her age and about her too. She needed to fulfil the formality only to gain their grant and they would do everything. According to Dolly, they were both seasoned and familiar with each other, and therefore, should not encounter any issues. They were in such a situation to run fast on the way of our conjugal life and be able to get its fruits. Dolly expressed all this to her mother.

Her mother began to think about the issue seriously. She also reported that she would convey her thoughts to her the following day. She agreed with her and communicated the message of Dolly to other members of the family.

The morning went and hours after evening came, usually. Dolly still hung around in suspense for the approval of her mother, while her mother still adhered to the perspectives of all the family members. Her mother called Dolly in the evening. And, she approached her and sat comfortably in her lap.

She stroked gently and spoke very gently, speaking to "o my darling Dolly! O, Dolly!" She said that she was a gentle girl, and so she should think about them...about the members of her family. She suggested she understand whatever her mother was saying. She said that they could not commit a second mistake in their life. As her elder sister had married a husband who they did not regard as suitable, it was no longer possible for her to avoid the humiliation. They did not like the love marriage. You also knew all this. Please do not repeat the same mistake. You know that only because of their eldest daughter some problems hit them. They roamed through the courts for many years in search of justice. They advised her not to do so, but her elder daughter did not listen to them. So now they were not in a situation to permit her to do so. She explained that they are social animals and must live in society, therefore, they must practice their traditions.

But listening to her, Dolly became angry. She seemed very sad and turned her face. While in the meantime it appeared that her happiness had been snatched away another person had "taken control" of her becoming a spouse. She thought that her mother was greatly mistaken, and she was right, and was unable to imagine that whatever her mother told her, was an attempt to make her happy and to provide for her future. But she did not understand and turning her face she began to mutter.

Dolly did not agree with her views. She was annoyed with her. She said that her mother did not want to see her happy. So, she would die – she would consume poison. She recommended that her mother adhere to it, while she would not. She said that she had her own life and her right; and she, therefore, wanted to live in her way. What was society? It was not above us. They had made it. It had not made them. So, they had a right to break it. She claimed that she would die, but marry no one else than Arran. According to her, her mother was living in the ancient age and Arran and Dolly lived in the modern age, and they knew its importance. Dolly suggested to her that if she wanted to live, she should live, but Dolly had not to live in such a state.

However, her mother was calm and still soothed her. Meanwhile, Dolly was very excited, she left the room and took position on a different sofa. So, her mother went to her and sat beside her. But she wanted to escape from there.

Having sat, she said very normally that no one listened to one's parents or guardians. One was one's, own master.

She raised some questions – where do you go? Where do you live? Who lives with you? Only you know. I do not know. Who is your guardian? Aren't you a ball of fire similar to your senior sister? The television is your guardian. We know nothing.

She said that Dolly spent the whole night in clubs without her permission, and now she wanted to befool them. However, they were not currently in a position to meet her. She was her daughter, and she could not say anything else. But she should think of herself. According to her, Dolly was a mortar. Her parents had gone on long enough to curb her, alas, they had only made that attempt so far in vain.

However, Dolly's mother was not able to marry without her consent because of the circumstances. She argued hard but failed. She reported that Dolly's big sister had spoilt her husband and now she wanted to spoil Arran. She was certain she would ruin herself and him by not obeying the guidance of her parents.

She was angry with Dolly and said to go away and repeat the past. She refused to say anything and she had nothing to view or review or interview. We wanted to be free from both of them.

She also said that she wanted to dispose of the false case against her husband, who was in jail unnecessarily. He was gentle and only because of her, he was suffering. She did not understand all this previously, so she lodged a false case against him, which was baseless and prejudiced. Just because of her prejudice, her husband and every member of his family were languishing behind bars under several clauses of the Dowry Act.

She was repenting of her bad deeds. She also stated that the Almighty himself could not forgive them for such a barbarous action done against them. Go away. They had long ago decided to drop the false allegation against them.

She admitted, shamefacedly, that they were not their daughters who were bringing down the family's glory. They said that both had defamed them. They were not in a condition to appear in front of people. Both of them were out of their control. One day, annihilation would take place. Their fourteenth year of age was the age of thunder and lightning. Their mother did not want to hide all this. "She crossed the line of morality according to her, and wanted to pollute the sacredness of marriage, just as the elder sister," as its dream was. Her mother said that God would never pardon her. One day, she would suffer from her evils.

Chapter - 12

I Am an Adult

Some months passed. Dolly was silent outwardly, but very active inwardly outwardly cool, but inwardly hot like the sun. She frequently remained silent. Sometimes, it happened that she did not speak with her mother. Sometimes, she did not eat at home. She spent her time in clubs and returned to her residence in the late hours of the night.

Sometimes, it also occurred that she remained absent from her home for a week. Her parents said not to go anywhere without their permission, but she threatened that she would consume poison. So, they were helpless and said nothing to her. They also sought the advice of their neighbours regarding her daily activities, but they expressed their helplessness in this regard. His neighbours said that the government had constituted a very strong law in favour of women, so no one could speak any word against women even a woman could not say any word against a woman right or wrong.

They said that they knew that no one could say any word to a woman because if he did so, he would be charged with sexual assault. He would be sent to jail, and he would be never released. He would die in jail. They said that they did not want to die in jail rather they wanted to live and die with their kith and kin. They said that hundreds of parents and husbands were murdered by their daughters and wives only because of sexual matters. So, they were not ready to help her and they would not interfere with Dolly. She was her daughter, and she had to consider the appropriate and/or inappropriate actions in her role as a mother.

So, the parents of Dolly were quite helpless. They regretted birthing a daughter such as her. They bewitched her the moment her mother got pregnant. They simply reported that God should indulge such bad boys who did not listen to their parents. It seemed that they were at the hands of a mighty soldier. They got very depressed, and they often did not eat. They also reported that there was no demand due to the pessimism caused by Dolly. They were just as irritated by her that they cursed her.

They said, "God may ruin your young age. God may spoil your life. You are the burden on this earth. You ignore the good advice of the parents. We were, in addition, just like, but everything we did was as instructed by our parents. We were not of free spirits. We used to think right and wrong...good and evil...social and unsocial. We were not blind like you. We also had those passions, but we used to perform only within the bounds of virtues. We never crossed its limits. That is the difference compared to that generation, here."

However, she did not want to hear her parent's advice. There was no impact of this on Dolly and she continued to do whatever she wanted. One day, her mother was cooking a meal alone. In the meantime, she went to her and informed her of her final decision.

She added, "I am an adult and there cannot be a "stopping" date for marriage, naturally. There is no matter of '14' or '18'. I feel I am an adult. So, I have the right to choose my path. I will obtain a certificate from any institution that states that I am "18" years old. Then the law will be also in my favour. I may just accept a helping hand from my friends if you say "no" to coming to my wedding ceremony. They are very helpful. You have to decide whether you are ready to fulfil the formality or not."

"You have to decide yourself," said Dolly's mother.

"Okay. I know to perform it...," she said.

Saying this, Dolly left her home and she met Arran to decide the proper date and place for oath-taking. They agreed and secretly performed the marriage ceremony at a temple. They were indeed successful in keeping it secret, but at the last minute, some people were privy to it. Abby was also informed of it very secretly because some people present in the temple recognized Arran and Dolly. Seeing them, some people were criticizing them, but some people were supporting their step. Senior citizens were receiving it as a stain upon society and the response was too bitter but adequate.

They said that they should look back for love. If they did not like to live together and did not know the meaning of conjugal life, they should die, and they should not try to defame the social institution of marriage. They were defaming it and digging a ditch for the coming generation, while no one had the right to do so or to pollute the holiest institution of society because all men passed through it one day. Arran and Abby had already fouled it and Dolly was currently engaged in it. They had ignored well-established social laws. Sex was a biological act after marriage for the continuation of the world. Hence, they are thereby well-defined systems so that one can get admission to it for a better tomorrow. The well-established system was the mother of fair and pure procreation, and fair and pure procreation was very important for a fair society. The system is universally known in every society, it applies to everyone, by everyone, and for everyone. Therefore, they should learn to regard it. However, rather than try to do just that, they were actively attempting to defame it.

Although there are some young and unmarried ones who rejected their opinions, they argued that society should not be treated in an open and free manner, but with their own thinking instead.

They said very flatly that marriage was a demand of the body, not of the society. Society was all for marriage, and the role of marriage was valueless. So, anyone had the right to do anything in any way for the fulfilment of his or her desire. All visitors should stay off the path to not harass or interfere with anyone. Even parents should not be disturbed in any way...they should not interfere. The mates not only had to live together their entire lives, but they also had to be free to decide their own fate. They had the right to write their fate.

They could consider one another better than others. Unfortunately, some parents interfered with the youth's affairs. Not surprisingly, youth had a right to experience and a right to love too. Enjoyment was the only way of salvation for youths. Meditation was nothing for them. It was for elderly men and women who were unable to appreciate sexual allurements. They were unaware of this divine and philosophic fact. Enjoyment was the main motive of life. Life was meaningless without it and life was absurd without it. To them, their principal medium of pleasure was intercourse, and light coupled with youth was a source of high-voltage current which could change the world. So, each youth had a right to flow his or her current according to one's will either right or wrong.

On the one hand, there were various views and reviews. However, Dolly and Arran were not yet ready to turn back. So, they started the oath-taking rituals in a temple. Abby was looking into the issue minute by minute and had already been informed by someone secretly. Say, when she arrived at the police station, she lodged a case against them.

According to Abby in her suit, she had only just been informed that her husband, Arran, was about to be remarried. He had continued to act up (be unruly) on her and break the law. He was committing a heinous crime against her. She did not want to lct him remarry. He will first have to meet her legal and social rights. She was dying of hunger. In contrast, he was planning to marry solely for the sake of it. That is, he was infringing upon the provisions of the *Hindu Marriage Act*. I understood the right time and right spot for them to take the oath. She said to go with the police to help and guide them for their arrest. She, therefore, begged the police to award justice to Abby.

The police were not permitted to linger, as the government made an order to take due measures against dishonest persons within one hour in cases relating to women. When the case was registered police went toward the spot; when Arran was about to put the holy vermilion on the forehead of Dolly, they reached that place and they were arrested for contravention of the Hindu Marriage Act in which there was a provision that it was illegal to marry if the wife was alive or husband was not a legal divorcee.

When Dolly was apprehended, she looked too gloomy, and it contained:

O world! O life! O time!
On whose last steps I climb,
Trembling at that, where I had stood before;
When will return the glory of your prime?
No more – oh, nevermore!

Out of the day and night
Joy has taken flight;
Fresh spring and summer, and winter hoar
Move my faint heart with grief, but with delight
No more – oh, never more.

Dolly's mind and heart filled with sorrow. She found her empty-handed. She received only criticism and squalor in her world. She started to recall her mother´s advice and to regret her step without knowing the result.

Arran was too upset and could not bear a single word to him. Both of them were taken to the police station independently. This news spread as fire and as the city's folk understood it, it reached the police station. A heavy crowd was seen. Abby was also there and savouring the crowd scene and the atmosphere surrounding it. In the meantime, she was very well, and she used to be rarely happy. She explained that she had followed through on her oath to teach Arran a lesson on litigation. In the meantime, she was quite savage and had been wearing a tight shirt and pantaloon. She was also using abusive words for them.

She said, "Heh, dog! Did you forget? I had previously told you to put me in jail and I have kept my promise. Will I die, and will you be able to enjoy your life with Dolly? Do you want to kiss Dolly and wound Abby? It is not possible. I will send you to hell. Do you not know me? I am fiercer than the sun and can scorch the universe. A woman can create; a woman can annihilate."

She said in a roaring way that Arran had perhaps not read the philosophical ideas regarding women. So, he should read it to know the womankind. She felt pleased to see tears in his eyes. Nobody any longer sought him out to console him with his tears. He would die in jail. No one would perform even his death rites. Their corpses will be thrown on the street and will satisfy the hunger of dogs. She told us that Arran and all of (her) other in-laws knew all of this. No one could bear the tears of a woman. No one could ignore this divine fact. A woman was a direct interpretation of a goddess. She said that her in-laws were happy when Arran worshipped Abby as a goddess; and as he behaved towards her as a puppet, sorrows undertook him. Now he could imagine the power of a woman. According to her, a woman was a goddess. She further indicated that she was a god/goddess, but was free to act nobly or wickedly for her pleasure and to play the game also involving her physical components.

While in the lodge silence reigned and it seemed as if he sought mercy, mercy and through mercy. Dolly is confined to another cage, yet she is no stranger to expression and coaxes forth her thoughts in an uninterrupted flow just like Abby. She was expressing her ideas boldly. She was cursing Abby too. In thc meantime, there were two women of two kinds one for and the other against.

Dolly declared that Abby was a witch who once ruined Arran and that she was ruining Abby's life now. She said that she had not snatched her husband. If Arran was her husband, Abby should live with him. She said that she was spending her life in nightclubs with her boyfriends. If Dolly was not prepared to cohabitate with him, can Dolly not cohabitate with him? Could she not marry him? What was wrong with it?

Dolly, before their case was registered against them, committed a crime against humanity. They were in a blissful place! But unfortunately, now they were in prison cells. Even god would not pardon her for her crime against them. According to her, God was not missing, and He would come to deliver His judgment not too far ahead and one day, they would get the justice they deserved.

In the meantime, it seemed that she was a philosopher. So many ideas were expressed by her. She could also be agitated, and sometimes she was like a quiet ocean. On the other hand, Abby was not ready to go back to her stand, and she continued to criticize them among the public and the media. They were listening to her in a most interesting and smiling inward way. She was enraged and her hair had fanned over her like a mask. She looked somehow different, and her face was a pale mask. Some well-wishers of Arran and Dolly prayed to Abby to drop the case against them, but she flatly refused to do so. Later a few of them recommended her for her clemency, but she toughened up and reprimanded them. She said that she wanted to see Arran weeping and dying. Her parents Doran and Lara were supporting her. Some people said that she was cruel. There is a saying that she was one of those products of contemporary culture.

A woman, who was in the scene, said that Abby was devouring womanhood, and her parents were taking part in it. She was obliterating her philosophies in service to women's liberation. That it was a woman was chivalrous and virtuous, but it was only bizarre. Her body language and dress revealed her strangeness, and her parents had watered her strangeness. Dignity should be preserved by everybody, but she was not in a position to hear anybody, she was exposing to the masses her naked body, and it was being taken in by the masses in terms of her naked physical attraction.

She told us what would be awarded her in court or with the police. Can the court or the police station, bring love, peace and rest to any man?

She then stated that the emotion of love was generated in the heart and in the mind of humankind. So, she should learn to live, not to litigate. In the beginning, she should control the situation. Now everything was out of her hands. Her understanding could bring happiness to her life. But she would get nothing here. She could show her look to the crowd. She was blaming the entire womankind.

This was not the true nature of any woman. Her parents were also uncultured and unaware of the realities of life and they were sponsoring her as she had beaten the other competitors. She had not even a single sign of womanhood. Her parents were of the same tray.

At the same time, she added that the police that one must also rethink the case. The police should be informed that she was not only unprepared to live with him but also unprepared to let anyone live in the name of the Hindu Marriage Act. This act was for man's benefit, and not to exploit anyone for it. No law allowed it. She is obliged to dispose of the case, with the aid of society and the law. They must do so. They would get nothing in the court or police station. Everything would be found in their understanding. They should know all this.

She was lamenting such laws which were inflicting more pain than pleasure upon a few. Heh, the Dowry Act...heh the *Maintenance Act*!

She raised a question. Is it possible to grant love, peace and, repose to the life of anyone if there is no communication between husband and wife?

She explicitly stated that the vast majority of cases (more than ninety-nine per cent) registered under these enactments were spurious and made up. There was an opposite truth concealed and cases were registered in their names. A shameful mistake was made by the court to dismiss the plaintiff, and judgements had to be made by the court under a law which was bloodless and spiritless, and quite merciless.

But Abby felt she was right, and her step was for the award of pleasure. He held her views in different ways and tried to show that she was quite right, and her husband was wrong. In the meantime, she was listening to her and grinding her teeth. It seemed that she would grind the old woman. Later, her reaction was harder than the former.

She stated, "They are not aware of the parliament's new law. Its name is the 'Women Exploitation Act'. They all have to read it, which is in every daily newspaper at the moment. According to the law, men who stand or remain for fourteen seconds next to a woman only are covered by the act. This is an offence and non-bailable. The law is with us...the parliament is with us...society is with us. We are a hundred per cent safe. There is no obstruction for women either we are right or wrong. Nothing in this world can harm us. No one can harm us..."

The lady warned our folk to keep a distance from that place and she declared she would make a complaint against them and they would end up in jail too. So, most of the people left the police station. Their attempt to compromise the case went in vain, while Arran was ready to talk on the issue and wanted to get her back to his home. But his attempt also went in vain. So, both Arran and Dolly were sent to jail.

Chapter - 13

Right or Wrong

Dolly and Arran wanted to take possession of the fruit of the wedding tree in a temple where thousands of marriages were performed, and such couples were living happily ever after indulging in conjugal bliss.

However, instead of them, Dolly and Arran received the consequences of being in prison. Their expectations were shattered. No way seemed clear to them. They would be powerless to act and forced to endure. Time had tightened them fully.

In contrast, Abby was having a good time with her worldly and choosy boyfriends in clubs until late into the night. In this way, three weeks passed. The well-wishers of Arran and Abby once again became active in the social solution of the issue. However, the audiences were not prepared to hear them. They seemed like a high-voltage electric current. So, no one dared to move for them.

After some days, a bail petition was moved in the court for Arran's bail and the counsel for the defence urged that his client was a victim of malice and prejudice of a woman like Abby, who was really out of the root of religion and duty. She had never been educated to live as a woman in the household. She was quite unaware of Indian culture and society. She considered life as a game to be played and wrong. No religion approved this practice of anyone. All holy books explained it very clearly. Salvation was the main motive of life. All people in India were aware of this fact and aware of the philosophy of life in the *Gita*. After marriage, the husband had not only one duty to fulfil the demands for his wife or himself, rather he had also to fulfil all other duties: social, religious, humane etc. The outcome was the establishment of a chasm between husband and wife, i.e., this chasm resulted in a misunderstanding between husband and wife. The same was the problem with Arran and Abby. He by no means had done anything wrong with his wife, and at no point in time did he want to harm his wife. He had fulfilled all of her requirements as a husband. However, she had misinterpreted him and so there is now a significant distance between them. This gap was filled with evils. She tried to ease her, yet she was too late to move on and the memories of her family conflict came back to back her. Hence, Arran was compelled to suffer mainly because of the *Dowry Act*, the *Hindu Marriage Act* and the *Women Exploitation Act*. These acts did not allow the legal authority to listen to the male side, but rather to the female side, and its bad effect was that women's feet were not on the ground of reality. They maliciously filed suits against men in the guise of the need for dowry. Several persons like Arran had become its victims each year in the country. The truth was another thing all of the time in such cases, but they concealed the truths in the pretext of those acts. Males were compelled to hear females, whatever they said. Not surprisingly, it was surprisingly ungenuine that a husband made the dowry by force, except in certain situations. In this kind of case, the learned Judge ought to apply his wit and his talent too. Here the fact was that Arran was not going to marry Dolly, rather he had been invited by her to participate in the wedding ceremony of her cousin. The council had its proof. But unfortunately, Abby could not understand the real matter and got a false case registered against Arran and Dolly, as the counsel said. This was a complete surprise that they were sitting there for their marriage. No law permitted them to suffer unnecessarily and illegally. He, therefore, begged the judge to grant bail for him under different sections.

The counsel of the prosecution, the same place, opposed the bail order.

He reported that his client, Abby, was a virgin. Her-in-laws were cruel and they tortured her usually. Its effect was that she was in despair and was longing to have her very natural desires fulfilled. She was starving and was already living with her parents, anyway. Now the fact was before the judge. Counsel agreed that Arran did indeed have an affair with Dolly and that he therefore wanted to keep Abby away from them. He needlessly inflicted pain upon her in the guise of an affair of the flesh (i.e., illicit love) with anybody, and that was unreasonable and whimsical. She was an honest woman, and there was no immorality anywhere, not even with anyone. He usually demanded dowry and tortured her. He wanted to marry Dolly secretly, but it was known by Abby. This was against the *Hindu Marriage Act*. He did not know the Indian culture and the law that no one could marry if his wife was alive. If his bail application was approved, he would impact the witnesses' testimony as well as the integrity of the investigation. He, therefore, begged the judge to dismiss his bail petition.

The Judge heard arguments from both counsel and the bail petition was denied.

"This is an example of the crime of a woman...exploitation and suppression of woman. None is allowed to do so. The court, therefore, dismisses this bail petition..."

In the meantime, Abby was present there. Listening to the decision of the court, she became very happy. On the other hand, the relatives of Arran were unhappy but very hopeful that the bail petition would be granted in the High Court. Immediately after one week, he moved an application for bail to the High Court. At the court, there was a discussion about the bail petition and it was given approval. So, he was released from jail.

However, Abby and her parent(s) never wished to see him at rest. Hence they filed two fresh suits against him and every member of his family as per different sections of the *Dowry Act* and the *Maintenance Act*. Under the *Dowry Act*, all the members of his family were accused, while under the *Maintenance Act*, Arran was only accused.

She claimed in court that she had been living with her parents for years. Her daughter was also living with her. Her parents were unable to fulfil her requirements. She was jobless and had no means of subsistence. She also reported being sick for many years. She also wanted to study. She, therefore, begged the judge to grant the maintenance for them under the *Maintenance Act*.

She further complained that her husband and all the members of his family tortured her. They beat her usually and demanded dowry. He demanded a *Ferrari* car. Her parents were unable to give it to him. Sometimes, he remained hungry because no food was given to her. She said that even a single loaf of bread was not given to her daily. Anyhow, she used to pass his time to in-laws. He says to bring Ferrari from anywhere and if she does not do so, he begins to beat her. Her parents had already given him two cars: an *i20* and a *Swift Dzire*, but despite all this, he was not satisfied with her and her parents. When she so said, she requested the judge to file a case against them under the Dowry Act.

Arran was noticed under the *Maintenance Act*. He received the notice and smiled, as one does with a love letter. It seemed that he had been habituated to so. Some people said that he had turned litigant.

Getting the letter, he smiled and said, "I will give her heavy maintenance as soon as possible. It is merely a dream for her. I will pay and she will enjoy? Is it possible?"

He also appeared at the court on the date of the hearing.

He urged in the court that that was the misuse of the *Maintenance Act*, and he was not in a situation to pay the maintenance for her livelihood because he was ready to live with her as husband and wife, and he had filed a case in the court for the restoration of his conjugal life. He was a good husband and did everything that was expected of him by his wife and daughter. She was a vagrant woman who wanted to marry again her paramour because this woman had a dalliance with other people. She falsely accused him and he viewed her as a domestic goddess. He loved her heartily. She had also fallen in love with her cousin's husband so she refused to live with him. Her parents were also misguiding her. She was an adulterous woman. There was nothing in the name of morality to her. She had only the pomp and show, and she was a storehouse of evils. She had enmity with virtues and Indian sensibility and with the feminine sensibility. She was a monarch of selfish thought and cared nothing about anyone. She was waiting to go back to his house and to forget the problems of his family. He, therefore, begged the judge to dismiss the case and issue an order for the restoration of his conjugal life.

Listening to his ideas, the Judge convinced both Arran and Abby separately to live together, but she was not ready to do so. The Judge, for example, sets the next date for the hearing.

This, at least, went by several dates with the Judge encouraging them all to live together and Arran was prepped to live together, but it was not her time to jump in. So, the Judge pronounced his judgement in her favour because she was entitled to get the maintenance for herself and her daughter.

"After a considered consideration of the respective arguments of the parties, the tribunal concludes that "the wife of Arran, Abby, is entitled to receive maintenance from Arran under sections...of the *Maintenance Act.* Arran will give out three thousand rupees for his wife Abby and her daughter's allowance every month. That amount would be deposited into her savings account every month...," the Judge delivered his judgement.

Getting the decision of the court, he was shocked, but she became very happy, and a sweet smile was easily visible on her face.

She expressed her pleasure, saying that she had already told him that she would get the money from him, and he would get nothing from her. Nothing! Not even a single kiss! However, she was his wife in the eyes of the law, as the law was for women and against men. Women never won and men never lost. He would earn and Abby would spend. He would see, and she would enjoy it. He would pine even for a single kiss. No girl would peep at him, but many boys moved around her because she had beauty...and she would have money. She thought that she would enjoy it and he would pay. She thought that he clearly understood the *Maintenance Act*. It was not enough. He would know everything in the future...under the *Dowry Act*. Abby said all this, listening to the judgment.

She expressed her ideas to her boyfriend very secretly, who belonged to her neighbour. Arran was looking at them very seriously, but Abby showed two fingers to him. When he saw a boyfriend with her, it became intolerable for him, and he ground his teeth and also wanted to move towards them to kill because it was quite intolerable that his wife was with her boyfriend. However, they did interfere with him too and advised him to go home. So, he said nothing and moved to his home.

Months passed. She continued to wait for the maintenance, and she frequently enquired into his bank account to know the balance, but in vain. So, her dreams were shattered and she became anxious. She became very sad.

After some months, she got a notice from the High Court and knew that he had appealed against the decision of the Lower Court.

Getting it, she got fired and began to abuse the whole male society. She stated that the males know how to take only the internal beauty of the females, and how to give nothing to them and they know how to pollute the females.

She said loudly that her age was growing fast. Her age of enjoyment was going to expire. He used her body for years before and after marriage, but now he did not want to give three thousand rupees per month to her as maintenance. She considered him a dog! She declared to straighten him whose use she had and had forgotten her entirely.

She was herself asking some questions. Now, who would ask me? Who will use me? The male society in its entirety has ruined the lives of the women in the society. Instead of the maintenance, I got a notice. Is this justice? Is this money? How will I live? Is this notice of my livelihood? Will it fill my stomach? That is, it appears that I shall not also receive justice in the law either. In my daily life, happiness, peace, and quiescence will originate from where?

In this way, six months passed. Time changed. The situation also changed. Her parents made her accountable for the family problems and blamed her for his/her pain. They longed to be away from their daughter, regardless of what. She began to live in a state of despair. As if the family discord in Arran's family had been absorbed into Doran's family. Either her parents were happy or unhappy, but they also approached the High Court. When the court heard for four sessions the court rendered its decision in her favour.

"Whatever maybe. But Arran is also obliged to maintain his wife Abby and her daughter. He will continue to credit three thousand rupees per month to her bank account from the 25th to the 30th of each month. He also has to pay arrears...Interest at the rate of 12 per cent per annum is calculated within 15 days from the disposal of the case. Once the above arrears have been paid, he shall accordingly notify this honourable court. There is no sound reason to file his petition in this court.

Having the court pronouncement in sight, she resumed knotting the threads of joviality not only her physical beauty but her very heart too filled with joy.

She said very laughingly, "Aha! Arrears! With 12 per cent interest! But I have finally got my justice and I will secure the compensation with 12 per cent interest from the date of the case admitted in the Lower Court. It will remove my all woes and sorrows and will bring happiness to my life. Aha, with 12 per cent interest! "

But on the other hand, Arran was not sad and very hopeful for his victory over time. Although he spent enough challenges in the past, he was unable to take on another burden/challenge. It seemed that his heart had been turned into stone, and he had become a man without tension.

He told, very solemnly, that it is what he would wish, to die, but never to render any type of maintenance toward her. He said that it was quite impossible, and she was living in the world of dreams.

He raised some questions is it possible that I will earn and she will enjoy? She will spend? How can a man not benefit from a woman?

Why does a husband not have the right to claim maintenance from his wife, if she refuses to move in together? Why? If both sides are the same, then why should the wife need to compensate? Why can a husband not get it?

He stated he would never obey in any way a law that has been made in favour only of women and also did not allow any chance for men to take a stand; it was a big question for masculinity. He thought a married woman also desecrated a man. So, he was also entitled to get maintenance. She would get old like a disreputable coat, but would never own it. He would also file a case against her in the Lower Court for the maintenance received. He stated that he was going to appeal to the Supreme Court against the verdict of the High Court. He also stated that he is willing to fight for men's liberation.

The following week he appeared before the Supreme Court to challenge the judgment of the High Court etc. He went to work with an affluent solicitor, a specialist in the field of this case. He proposed that Arran should waive the item in court because, in the court, the item would become long in his life, and his life would go on litigating.

He explained that family business should not be taken to court if it was not so important, and it should be settled at the social level because the court was unable to determine or direct any family to get along well and live happily morally and socially. It was a matter of understanding. During the long period of the court, something new happened, and some of the matters were further complicated. A distance between wife and husband was created. That was his experience as a man and as a lawyer. There were so many examples of this type. Both spouses should be taught to live in a tranquil state of rest and peace. It was also quite clear that the male side had to pay the maintenance to her at any cost or in any condition.

The counsel said, "She may be virtuous, or she may be characterless. Whatever may be! Right or wrong! Corrupt or gentle. Or she has an extramarital relationship with several persons. No male is exempted from any conditions. She has to prove only one thing, that she is one's wife. The male is not in a position to deprive her of the maintenance under the Maintenance Act."

However, Arran was not anxious, but comfortable there. And he was positive about this, saying, nothing would go wrong with him. He was very hopeful for his bright future.

He said that he knew he would have to pay the maintenance to her and no one could save him. Nothing would be gained by him in this case. But he had come to the honourable court only to linger it as it was possible by the counsel in this lengthy process of the court so that she would die or would turn mad without getting it. If they lingered, she could become mad, or she could herself die.

He said, "If she dies, who would claim? Will she get it easily? Impossible! Such cases are not rare and there are many examples of this kind in which the respondents died due to depression and tension. Some committed suicide. Some of them grow old. So I tell you I'd like you to hold out for it anyway and I will find you a solution within it."

So, the case was drafted and filed too. Filing the case in the Supreme Court upon his arrival home, he immediately reached out to one of the most celebrated lawyers of the local court. He sought his legal advice. He advised him to/or rather, he recommended filing a lawsuit in the local court. He became ready to do so and file a new case in the Lower Court. The case was made and filed by his lawyer then and there. Arran was highly optimistic that he would win the case and would be awarded maintenance from Abby, while some predicted he would receive nothing in the case other than the passage of time and expenditure on money which had been accrued in the hospital, by taking improper steps.

He claimed in the court, "He starved to death as he had been always suffering from years of illness. He had no source of income. He was unemployed. Due to his disease, he also stopped practicing medicine. Currently, he has no job. His wife was not living with his wife but was living with his parents. Only a widow was willing to marry him since Abby had disgraced him and his purity. No one was there to take care of him and his ageing parents at his residence. He had the right to live as well, just as any other people had. So he, accordingly, prayed to the court to give him thirty thousand rupees, every month, as maintenance, under different articles."

The case was admitted to the court. Thus, two years flew through the Supreme Court for justice. The petitioner attempted to delay the proceeding because of disease and other reasons. Date by date for hearing in the court…counter…rejoinder…the first date...the second...the third and so on. Arran was mentally prepared not to pay the maintenance to her; and on the other hand, Abby was impatiently waiting to get it - for getting the maintenance per month and arrears with 12 per cent interest since the date of the admission of the case in the Lower Court.

Abby still waited for the maintenance and arrears, at 12 per cent interest annually. She received a summons from the Supreme Court a few months later. Both the parties approached there. In this way, the months passed.

A new turn came to Arran's life. He was sleeping at night in his home. In the meantime, the police came to him, and he was arrested under the sections of the Dowry Act. He was sent to jail. His previous parents and other family members were not arrested as they did not leave their homes and thus took an active role in the wedding ceremony.

The next day, a bail motion was filed before the Lower Court regarding the bail of this individual, but it was refused. However, his parents and relatives were not hopeless and in a week, they applied to the High Court and his bail was allowed. So within eight days, he was released from jail.

After his release, some of their well-wishers held a social meeting and decided to dispose of the issue in any way. A few of them reached Arran, however, he flatly refused to discuss the matter with them. They tried to soften him but in vain. He promised that he would die or would live without a wife and would die issueless, but would never accept her as his wife because she had spoiled his life. They were, therefore, quite helpless, and they went back without any type of discussion. Time continued to pass, but no solution was seen. They were living in their ways. After some days, some other people contacted Arran first. They proposed that he should ignore the history of family conflict. And they said to him that it does happen sometimes in any of the life of an individual, and he must start anew his life in a new way. However, he was not in a position to speak with them and shot them down outright.

So they phoned up his parents and explained that they would wish to take up the question of Arran. However, they were not prepared to do so and outright refused to intervene in Abby or Arran in relation to the problem. They reported that they were remarkably helpless to act independently and the problem was out of their grasp. They were very frustrated.

They said that Arran was beyond their control. Abby was beyond the reach of their minds. These boyish men of this age group stood out of reach, everybody.

They raised some questions there. What do they do? When do they do? Why do they do this? How do they do? Everything is beyond our reach – out of control. God knows only. Arran has to think, what should be done? What should not be done?

Moreover, they said that Arran had to be silent and they would be silent. According to them, Arran was a king of self-will. The whole generation was of this type. He listened to him for nothing when he decided to marry Abby. He decided himself and did so. His parents participated in the wedding ceremony only. There was no role of his parents. They suggested he not marry her because they knew that she was not under the control of her parents and moved anywhere with anyone before her marriage, and there was nothing to her in the name of sacrament and virtues. She desired to do that same thing over and over again after she got married, which was out of the question for any family. So, the whole family was overtaken by the strife, and they were compelled to suffer. They had only tears and they bled. Woes and sorrows had embraced them. It seemed that they would never go out of their clutch.

The parents of Abby were listening to them carefully, and they knew that there was no easy solution to the problem, but one thing felt that there was a change in their stand, and they wanted the solution to the problem.

They also posed some questions for them. Will you protest Arran's decision? Will you accept Abby as a daughter-in-law? However, they were remarkably silent, and it was obvious that the solution to the problem lay, right under their silence.

And when they realised that there was a ray of a solution in their silence, they reached out to Abby and tried to melt her. They proposed to her that this was part and parcel of life and could be fixed with just understanding, such as a car that is broken and then starts correctly, 'often after seeing a mechanic'. But she was not ready to change her stand. She refused to discuss anything regarding the issue.

Very flatly and gruffly, she went on to say that, subsequently, she did not want to see the least bit of anything to do with the latter, and she certainly did not want to see his face. He was her enemy who fired her life...her young age. He spoiled her beauty. She also reported that other people wanted to marry her. They were in rows to gain her. She wants to die (but she would never go to him) because she has never been able to leave the past of discord (the past of violence and atrocities) behind and not only peace ever in her life. She, therefore, never wanted to look back to lick the spit. Going there is equal to licking the spit. It is impossible for her.

Having all that, she started chanting a lyric in a melodious way as follows:

The sun may rise in the west;
The moon may become too hot;
The sun may become too cold;
The earth may change its rounds;
Wind may stop to blow;

The sun may move around the earth;
Nature may change itself;
The desert may melt fully;
Rivers may stop flowing;
Snow may become too hot;
Rose may discharge a bad smell;
Apples may become bitter;
Thorns may turn into flowers;
Dears may eat meat;
Tigers may eat grass;
All may become possible.
Abby is the Creation – nature too,
I will never turn to him;
Cannot accept, Arran as my husband;
Cannot go to his shade;
I can't let him keep his arms on me.

Listening to this lyric sung by her, they kept their hands on their heads. But despite all this, they did not lose their patience and contacted her parents for a solution. The reaction of her parents was neither for nor against. They claimed that Abby would decide all the information, and none of them confirmed that they talked about the problem. Their despair of the issue was easily felt.

Accordingly, time slipped by month after month, until the year was almost upon them. But no solution came to them. Both Arran and Abby were each stitching on their trajectory and flitted about freely, just as the output of high-power machines with no bogies. Yes! Without bogies! They were quite chainless. No sign of their conjugal life was felt. As their [tried] attempts at allaying them failed, a certain group of the social organization sought their attention and offered them to look for the re-establishment of happiness, love, peace and repose for their life. They visited them regularly. On the hearing day, they also occasionally went to the court. They persuaded them in various ways, using multiple examples of the same city. They were also prepared to be accountable in case of casualties under the existing legal provisions. Sometimes, they also visited their homes to convince them. They also were prepared to bestow them only if they obeyed them. But despite all this, no solution came to them, and they continued to do it in their ways and moved freely.

Meanwhile, Abby received a notice from the Lower Court that her husband had filed a suit for claiming maintenance. Getting the notice, she laughed and said that he needed sexual maintenance.

She said, "...can a husband get maintenance from his wife? Never! There is neither provision in nature nor the law. A woman loses her virginity at the hands of a man. She has a right to the maintenance and it is part of the law, too. But no maintenance is given to a husband because nothing is lost by him at a woman's hand. Has male virginity? He has no purity...no virginity. Virginity remains in a woman. A woman is a symbol of the Creation...she is a goddess."

Those who were at the scene said nothing to her, but they talked about it. They reported that, on the condition that she looked at the woman as representative of the Creation...a symbol of the goddess, and virginity remained in her, she should maintain its honour at any cost..., but she defamed the society and its institution.

Chapter - 14

All Ends Well

Time passes, as it continues to pass forever. However, it seemed to them that it flew by too quickly. Both Arran and Abby could not grasp its worth. Their parents were also unable to command them. The sense of despair had also overtaken them. They felt helpless at the hands of fate or chance.

Arran had become entangled in the affairs of the world and had suffered from illness for many years. He, therefore, consulted some other doctors for his treatment. They suggested keeping himself away from strife as it was possible for him.

He obeyed them and enrolled to do a postgraduate (such as a Master in Fine Arts) study in Fine Arts College, Kashi. He took the course for two years and graduated. Some days later he set up the painting workshop and painted some figures of gods and goddesses, politicians, landscapes, etc. His painting was liked by people and they admired him. They said that his painting was sort of the same as that of Picasso. So, some people began to call him 'Picasso II'. He became famous for his paintings, and he said that he would donate the last breath of his life to painting. He also painted his nostalgia and strife, but he did not comment on the issue of strife.

With time, he transformed into a national-level painter and earned numerous prizes. However, it appeared as though the festering wound of family quarrel had been closed by his work of art and he had waived the matter of dispute. He never talked of any concept regarding his marital relationship.

'Indian Culture and Civilization' was her special paper in examinations. This paper made a total change to her and she was revitalized. She released numerous albums that were related to her special paper which made her a well-known singer. She only then became a national singer after several years. She sang many folk song lyrics in many radio studios of All India Radio. She also won several national-level awards. As soon as she uttered those words the folk songs had superseded her Indian Culture and Civilization making her then the most beautiful daughter of the Indian Culture and Civilization, not only a biological daughter of Lara and Doran.

She said, "...I am one of the loveliest daughters of India and Indian Culture and Civilization. I used to be about beauty, for beauty and in the name of beauty. Now I am for Indianness, of Indianness, and through Indianness. I am completely satisfied with what I have at the moment..."

She also never stated her position on the family fighting and it looked like she knew absolutely nothing about the extent of the fight.

A new turn came to their life the 'U' turn came to their life. There was a famous monastery at the foot of the Himalayas known as the Peace Centre. There was a saint who lived in it. His monastery was very holy in India. Some people went there in good humour and devoutness and received a blessing from the saint. Arran also started going and preaching to his church. The saint delivered his preaching daily to his devotees. They listened to him and raised some questions if necessary. He replied to their queries, providing several illustrative examples from the religious scriptures. There was also a connection to the network, with some followers linked online to it or at least via video conferencing. His sermons were printed in the daily newspapers of the monastery and there were enough of its readers. Some people regarded the monastery as a place for pilgrimage. Some regarded it as a spiritual centre. This religious site of spiritualism forced its practitioners to get to the heart of things or to the truth.

Arran went there often and carefully listened to his sermons and also tried to adjust his workday to his life. Later, he became a lifetime member of the newspaper of the monastery. He read it daily. So, there was a wide impact of spiritual ideas on him, and he moved towards spiritualism.

The next day, Abby also received a monastery newspaper and looked at it carefully. She liked the newspaper very much. The ideas of spiritualism affected her. Thus, she started buying one of its copies per day. She later, as a life member of the journal became its reader unwinding each day. In the process, she experienced a broad effect and became spiritualized. She even started to go to the monastery to attend the preaching of the saint. But both Arran and Abby did not know one another's visitor participation.

One day, for example, he was at the pulpit and a woman came forward to discuss a specifically personal issue with him. While Abby was in the same seat and listening to them. Afterwards, she also rose up and presented her trouble in front of him.

She said, "O Baba! Please show light to me. Enlighten me. My life is full of troubles. I bleed. I have been wounded. Please bless me...award a boon to me."

"Live gladly! Everything will be good for you. God will protect you. He protects all of us. Bliss will take the place of your miseries. God is in your soul. You have to listen to Him. You have to understand His language and activities. God is by everybody's side watching everybody that is by everybody's side."

On the other hand, the members of the social organisation were watching over them regularly, and when they knew that there was a new turn to the life of Arran and Abby, they once again made their attempt to soften them to get them back to their peaceful and joyful conjugal life. They also met their parents for the same and knew that there was a ray of hope for the solution to their problem. Hence, they started to toil on that very beam of light of hope and began to ply the yarn of peace, repose, and happiness.

On the one hand, they made the ground ready for dialogue, and they set up a family meeting, secretly in an inn. Arran, Abby and their parents were called there. They handled the issue very minutely. In the first place, they instructed Doran that her true parents had been that woman's parents and to shoulder the role of her father as her creator or maker for her to be happy. He became very emotional, and it seemed that he was a tired soldier at the hands of his enemy.

He cried very emotionally that he had been guilty of many crimes…several mistakes in every walk of his life. He was, at that moment, senseless and deprived of the right to suffer. He never wished to hear again the crying of his daughter, for it is nothing that anyone desires. However, they had followed the line of verse that was written in weeping and wailing a line which was full of wild thorns and precipices. Despite all this, if they said, he agreed with them. He further enjoyed telling his daughter to make her life decision which was legally proven by the religion, duty, culture, society, sacrament and Hindu philosophy. No one had the right to fire our culture. She had to select one among two options either she would go to her own home or she would remarry.

But as she listened to the word 'remarry', she became very emotional and said, "No! I will never do so. I will never remarry. I will never defame the social institution of marriage. I will never spoil the roots of tradition roots of virtues. It is quite impossible. Impossible! None should think that I will remarry."

She continued to say that she had no right to ill-fame the tradition of an Indian woman. Then for her, an Indian woman was regarded as a symbol of the Creation a symbol of Nature. The Hindu marriage system was a super-social system in the world. She had made a lot of errors, and she felt she no longer wanted to go on. No longer does she hesitate to express that she wants to turn back and look back to that happy married life. She was ready to embrace her husband, and she wanted to forget the past the past of the family strife. She was ready to go at his hands. Regretting the mistakes of the past which led to their past misunderstanding, she was understandingly prepared to embrace his embrace for the rest of their lives. Her love is immortal.

She could not live without him. She was incomplete without him. Thus, this was a revelation for Abby. She was late but right.

Listening to it, they admired her. Arran was also present there, but he said nothing.

They stated "Abby had succeeded Indian girl tradition," i.e. She was late but right. What was evident from this point onward was, that woman was then the Creation, and the destruction as well. She held both types of power she could create and she could annihilate, too. Hence, she was Nature…she was the Creation. This was the reason and therefore she was taken as an emblem of Power. Abby was ready to create heartily. She had understood the reality of life. Obscurity had gone. Her eyes were able to see right or wrong her spirit was able to understand right and wrong. They continued, "Man is also equal to a woman who moves with her step by step. He is a machine that draws the Creation, and that machine comes from a woman. This is the difference between man and woman."

They, later on, went to Arran and said, "Now you should go forward to bear his worldly realities. He ought to support her wrists, a duty for all mankind, well, men. As soon as any woman thinks of a man, the man gives way to defend her. This is the tradition of male-kind in the world. History is its eternal witness."

Arran hesitated to say anything. He was astonished by the alteration in her behaviour. There was no moment seen to his body. He remained quiet and they were all sitting in their line of sight with their heads in their hands.

After some moments the parents of Arran said that they had continued to say to both Arran and Abby that love, peace, rest and happiness were neither produced in fields nor televisions or mobile phones. All of this, instead, was generated within the mind and the heart of man. But they did not listen to them. Their children always wanted to be happy, but they are now bringing the legacy of their hard work to fruition. Arran had to decide whether he had to prop the hands of Abby or he had to remarry.

"I will make it clear next Sunday," said Arran.

So, the family meeting was postponed to next Sunday.

The next day he went to the saint and told him his thoughts.

"O, Baba! I am wounded. Joy has gone far away from me."

"Joy's right there, you've got to experience it."

"But...O Baba! It has been unseen for more than eight years."

"Joy visited you on a few occasions, but you swatted it away. And then you'll have it in your hands," says it.

"But from where?"

"It is produced in your spirit."

"The other day, a family meeting took place and my wife, Abby is willing to the owner to come", etc. At the time, she was not prepared to live with me and several reports of our respective problems have been filed. Will the woman, who ruined my life, be able to live peacefully with me?"

"When one is governed by good angels, one performs good works. Now she is governed by good angels. So, she will perform good works."

"However, I disbelieve her when I think back to the days I spent with her."

"Over time, everything has changed."

"What will be got by me?"

"There is no matter of getting or losing. You will have the same as is received by the other in this world."

"But I do not believe her sudden change."

"Everything is changed over time..."

Since I am afraid of her now and do not like the conjugal life, I became the unique one on Earth.

"That which passes the conjugal life also fulfils all the rights of a man. The person, who serves others, also serves God. Man's service is God's service."

"I have listened to many men about love, but it was never felt by me, even in my conjugal life. I don't know who is now, ever for me. From where will I gain love? "

"Love produces all the virtues of mankind such as mercy, sympathy, compassion, cooperation, brotherhood, humanism, etc. However, a set of social, worldly ignorant people do not know the original meaning of love. Love is spiritual. Lust is not loved. Love comes from the spirit, whereas lust comes from the body. Love is spiritual, while lust is physical. Look back for love."

"O, Baba! You have enlightened me. Now I understand the true nature of love. This is the future way in which we will dwell in an ambience of love, harmony and tranquillization. It will be free from lust. The next full moon day, I will embrace her forever."

Through being told or learning it, Abby is very happy. Then her happiness was uncontrollable.

Here, in this state, she wrote to Arran, her husband, "What joy there is in spring after winter! What a lovely, peaceful arms you are after so many tides and gales! Oh, my spirit! O, my love! O, my sweetheart! Your immortal face as a star is my only light. Now, forever yours."

When Arran received this message, he immediately sent his own message to Abby, "O my divine spirit! Morning is fresh and pleasant after night. Our love is without bond, and I wish you close to me when I move towards the blissful seat in heaven."

Chapter - 15

Now, Forever Yours

Through all the disasters, Arran wanted to embrace Abby one more time, and she also wanted him. Dying in his lap was her wish, and a similar wish she had with her eyes that Arran also wanted. This shows how true their love was after many years, and it was quite unexpected.

Arran's positive reaction was not because of some deep-hearted passion but because he was completely ruined due to litigation. He wanted to live with her while ignoring the fact that there was a tragic past with her. He still was very sick with the litigation as Abby had used the law against him distorting the judicial image of the court. Several cases were instituted against him and his parents by Abby and were still ongoing in various courts. He was also jailed.

Arran's parents were literally dumbstruck by Arran's choice to accept her again. They had taken Abby's re-entry to be the next chapter in the sorrows of their lives. They said that it is preferable to live without a son and a daughter-in-law who with each passing minute created problems and destroyed the peace and rest of the family. They told Arran to make up his mind and do as he wished to; whether he wanted to rejoin with Abby or not. They openly told them that they would live apart from their son Arran and daughter-in-law Abby.

Arran also consulted his friends on whether to accept his parents' objection and disagree with Abby's past. His friends also insisted that he shouldn't take her back. It would be hazardous for him and his family.

They said, "This will be the greatest spoiling of your whole life if you accept a woman who spoiled your life and ruined the peace and rest of your family. Because of her deed, the family lost its good name as of yore... In our lives, we have been officially battered and abandoned by our brothers and sisters just to stand by you in saving the brutality and lies of Abby. If you accept her, she won't change her – her habit will remain the same. You would rather die alone than a woman who has nothing to back up and no virtue at all..."

Arran, in a confused state, had no thoughts of what he should do. On the other side, Abby waited for the date fixed by them for her to receive. Her parents were really eager to send her to in-laws, also because they had lost respect due to the desecration of Abby being exposed.

Media raised two issues very frequently. One issue was Niki-Atus; the other was Jaya-Ray. These would shock the entire existing system of marriage, relationship, and social ties, and news articles about them were cast frequently in all leading newspapers and electronic media; people discussed these issues on buses and trains, at crossroads and in shops and offices, just about everywhere: in every family and with every friend. While most of them were fearful of these issues, they expected that this could also happen to them or their families.

Thus, the Jaya-Ray issue was an everyday event and gave overbearing media coverage. Everyday spelt headlines of all leading youth hubs and media channels. Each day, police or other investigating agencies brought out some fresh issues regarding them. The police disclosed the murder of Ray and that his wife Jaya was under arrest for that. People became furious with the inordinate delay in the proper action against her, and upon exerting pressure, she was arrested for the murder of Ray.

Police said, "One night Ray was sleeping, and Jaya and her lover Bora killed him. Jaya had accepted her guilt and also turned in the weapons and other things used for his murder..."

This development also forced Arran to reconsider his decision to accept Abby. Many people said that the message she sent Arran to live with him was part of a conspiracy to kill him quickly. Many people felt it was a sensitive issue and recalled the former wife's murders. Several husbands had awful thoughts and felt uneasy at night in the bedroom with their wives. They said that Arran's response to the text was solely out of pity for her because of her suffering as a result of false litigation against him. They told him never to think about accepting Abby again.

With this, Arran, who did not think much about what to do, also became perplexed and lost. Another case of Nikki-Atus came into the limelight when Nikki's husband committed suicide because, as he shared, of frequent torture by different courts so filed by a couple of his wives. The court was taking charge of the false pleadings, and opposite to this, the court passed several discriminatory orders against him, viewing the charges laid against him by Nikki under the Dowry Act, the Maintenance Act, and the Domestic Violence Act. People were unhappy with the courts. They said that the court was a great tool to torture the husbands in their false cases against the wives but never bent an ear to the husband's pleadings.

Arran suffered under the false accusations made by his wife, Abby, against him and his parents, aimed at torturing them in the name of law. So, he was further confused and frightened about his decision to live with Abby.

There were numerous protests and meetings against what they had termed the misapplication of the law and lack of concern from judges. They marched all over the country demanding the abolishing of acts where the only evidence was the lie that the husband tortured her by demanding dowry, after which the husband would be called to account and further penalized. The agitation processions and many marches against the lawmakers attracted the attention of the government to reconsider these laws. This prompted the government to constitute a committee to go into the law in question and recommend the necessary amendments.

There was a committee of five retired judges of the Supreme Court, to which a report was made thus:

- The Dowry Act has accordingly given rise to a culture of false accusations; cases abound across India, and the entire judiciary has now been put at risk of disrepute.
- With improper deeds shown in a marriage, the disharmony between the spouses spills into disorders between the cousin wives and all the family's other relations. These wives coerce their husbands and create counterfeit cases against their spouses for reasons such as adultery, sexual exploitation, torture, assault, violence, and demands for dowry money and other material resources.
- Sadly, the scandalous law of the Dowry is no more than an instrument of terrorized and soulless wreckage – a bloodied, immoral mode for doing grievous things to a husband and his family and a cause for wholesale killings.
- There are absolutely no provisions for the protection of husbands. They are without any remedy to live and secure justice all the time since the due process of law, hearing in courts – futile all times with far landed-away judgments and orders – take years and years for false cases, loss of other potential responsibilities, hazards of livelihoods: both physical and emotional, happy endings deny them any degree of continuation in life and instead shower them with immense loss, indignities, suffering, torments, social disrespects, and more humiliation.
- Because of the authoritarian, illegal, unethical, impractical, nihilistic, terrifying, derogatory, and notorious laws, thousands of husbands are left with no other options than to commit suicide.

- Citizens often call the attention of politicians, clergy, and others who should represent society to trampling on their rights if they have been tortured, harassed, or humiliated.
- To artificially create dependency, for securing grants, this Act is delightfully and dexterously misused. One is to earn while the other is being enjoyed – to create a class of unemployed. Today, it has become a fashion not to make adjustments and weaken family threads, but rather fake statements and, in consequence, malign the entire judiciary for their poor judgements.
- These acts have created enough problems for the whole nation. This act simply is one that creates people only to remain dependent on others and they only learn how to loiter a nuisance inside empty halls.
- As far as some provisions in this regard are concerned, nothing like that is found outside our country. Some people have just a limited time to set up and start their own lives in a different way.
- Many women have balanced the Coopers Act in their favour and marry with the idea that in marrying that spouse, they can benefit their family. Each month sees the filing downtown of new allegations against their husbands with new demands for consideration and for the ruin of all.
- Women say openly in family courts: He will earn and we will enjoy.
- Cases of this nature should only be permitted to be filed in the family courts of their jurisdiction or the family courts of the most neighbouring district courts; the plaintiffs should never be permitted to choose where to file first.
- Here, the government was not supposed to give the right for anyone to do such things that benefit illegally and lead to someone in a crooked way.
- The government needs to realize that if a plaintiff files a case in Kanyakumari and the opposite party resides in Kashmir,

they will have to travel a great distance to see the case in court, which was falsely filed against them.

- The Domestic Violence Act is increasingly misused. Women looking for any reason to separate from a husband who has nothing but their own best interests at heart claim all sorts of harassment, and false cases are brought against the husbands.
- This convinces the husbands never to accept such troublesome wives who levelled false cases against them. It becomes a matter of honour for him: he ends up spending all his time in court instead of earning a livelihood.
- These acts must then and there be amended for the sake of people all over the country and shall operate on all the cases already running in different courts under that act.
- So, the committee recommends amending the Dowry Act for the sake of the people of India and its culture and human rights – to fill up the gap between wives and husbands, and finally – the committee recommends that the Domestic Violence Act be amended in such a way that it does not misuse and get away with false cases to malign the purity of the judiciary system.

Considering various aspects, the committee has concluded that mass misuse has been made under such acts, which has brought the entire system of our country to its knees. Numerous families were disintegrated: some men and women committed suicide; many were dragged in and out of the court instead of earning a living. The court campus was also in an atmosphere of blackmailing and bargaining for such women in return for favours.

This report was forwarded to Parliament, bypassing the government's offices, with a promise to discuss the report and take necessary action at the earliest possible moment.

At the same time, the government appointed a five-member committee to amend the rules that caused such misuse by either party under such acts. The regulations were revised, applicable to all such cases running already in various courts under the respective acts, and the demands of the committee were satisfactorily met by the government.

It hit the newsstands and media. People bought the papers and exclaimed their astonishment at such a conscious legislature which put a blanket amendment upon such rules that had ruined the lives of millions through false cases. With this, people let out a sigh of relief, expecting that misuse of such laws would cease from now on. The government also widely publicized the amended acts, which was such that hardly a new case had been filed in the court since then. There was a decline of 97 per cent in such cases under those acts that year since they knew well that if they connived at lodging a false case, they would not win.

The latest news – too much heinous and heart-rendering – also affected the minds and hearts of Abby and Arran. The news struck the nation like a punch to the gut, an awful thud that echoed through every household, heart, and home – the murder issue of Saur – the horrifying issue of Saur-Musk. The name itself resonated with unimaginable horror, and it was not simply a murder, but a careful piecing together of a life, of a love, of everything precious and dear. The details, which were initially murmured and later splashed screams in the headlines, were grotesquely surreal – the husband, dismembered and murdered by the person that once pledged to love him, killed in a sick dance of cruelty with her lover. And for the final insult, he was cut into pieces and laid to rest in a drum of sand, cement, and concrete.

A feeling of disgust, a tidal wave of justified rage, flooded the country. The mind of the nation recoiled in terror at the awful rawness of the deed itself. It cuts across gender and status. Men, fathers, sons, and husbands saw their own frailty in the awful death of Saur. Women, mothers, daughters, and wives experienced the shameful pain that one of them could have committed this barbarity.

The atmosphere was charged with anger. Editorials emerged in the local newspapers, demanding justice and pleading for a punishment that would eventually, even if only slightly, redeem the severity of the assault on Saur. Even the internet – the usual cesspool of trends and outrage – became an arena for rage to express itself. Memes, which are usually the art of humour, emerged into blunt statements of condemnation, each picture a pixelated scream at the incredible darkness that descended upon Saur. Each report, each comment, and each angry emoji was imbued with a sense of communal grief and desire for vengeance.

The air was thick with anger. Editorials were printed in the local newspapers that begged for justice and asked that punishment be meted out that would try to, if only minimally, atone for the horrendous assault on Saur. Even the internet, a cesspool of offence and trending outrage became an outlet for unvarnished rage. Memes that historically have served as going jokes have mutated into unfiltered statements of condemnation, each image a pixelated yell at the incredible darkness that has consumed Saur. Each news story reposted, each comment posted, and each angry emoji posted was filled with feelings of communal mourning and desire to even the score. Its trial process was going on according to the new laws.

The amended trial process was to apply to cases pending under these acts. Thus, Arran and Abby were also summoned so that their new petitions could be filed if they so desired.

That was the moment when he was summoned. Although she had first sought to get hold of her husband Arran to consider settling these cases, Arran had neither time nor interest in her hidden intentions. All sweet talk could not alter her desire to spoil the remaining years of Arran's life along with the life of his family members. Arran was also confident of getting justice out of the amendments once made in these acts.

The court gave them a week's time within which they were to settle their issues amongst family members and relatives under the supervision of the Village Headman, failing which the court would commence the new trial under amended acts.

The well-wishers of both families gathered to resolve their issues, but it was to no avail. Arran remembered all those dreadful events and declined to take her in again.

In other words, both sides filed their petitions with new amendments and were scheduled to hear the arguments day by day. It took three days to complete the trial, and the court was to announce its verdict based on merit. Abby, in her plaint, requested the court to restore her conjugal rights because she was guilty and begged for pardon for her acts. Arran prayed to the court to dissolve the marriage because she had destroyed him and the whole family by framing various false charges against them.

The court would give its judgement on the eighteenth day of the next month after which both were ordered to remain present.

The eighteenth of the month – the date of judgement of the fate of Arran and Abby. Abby was serious and Arran was happier than ever before and he expected justice under the amended acts. Abby arrives at the court with her parents in an unusual manner. She prayed before the judgement to pass an order to live together. She also filed a self-signed bond to hand over to Arran. Her parents also requested the court for the same.

She urged, "I know there is a solution to every problem and every war ends with a peace treaty. However, I know I committed several mistakes ignoring all the facts because of my misunderstanding. I beg your pardon. Marriage is not a joke, but a life dealing with all the realities in every situation at any cost. Now, there is a total change in my spirit and I want to spend the entire part of my life with Arran forgetting the past. So, please, for the sake of my hearty explorations, award an order to Arran to accept me just now, and hand over my signed bond to Arran entitled, *Now, Forever Yours*."

THE END